hurricane
song

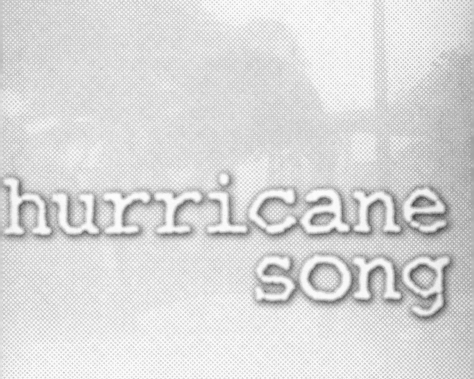

hurricane song

PAUL VOLPONI

VIKING

VIKING
Published by Penguin Group
Penguin Group (USA) Inc., 345 Hudson Street, New York, New York 10014, U.S.A.
Penguin Group (Canada), 90 Eglinton Avenue East, Suite 700, Toronto, Ontario, Canada M4P 2Y3
(a division of Pearson Penguin Canada Inc.)
Penguin Books Ltd, 80 Strand, London WC2R 0RL, England
Penguin Ireland, 25 St Stephen's Green, Dublin 2, Ireland (a division of Penguin Books Ltd)
Penguin Group (Australia), 250 Camberwell Road, Camberwell, Victoria 3124, Australia
(a division of Pearson Australia Group Pty Ltd)
Penguin Books India Pvt Ltd, 11 Community Centre, Panchsheel Park, New Delhi—110 017, India
Penguin Group (NZ), 67 Apollo Drive, Rosedale, North Shore 0632, New Zealand
Penguin Books (South Africa) (Pty) Ltd, 24 Sturdee Avenue, Rosebank, Johannesburg 2196, South Africa

Penguin Books Ltd, Registered Offices: 80 Strand, London WC2R 0RL, England

First published in 2008 by Viking, a member of Penguin Group (USA) Inc.

3   5   7   9   10   8   6   4   2

LIBRARY OF CONGRESS CATALOGING-IN-PUBLICATION DATA
Volponi, Paul.
Hurricane song : a novel of New Orleans / by Paul Volponi.
p. cm.
Summary: Twelve-year-old Miles Shaw goes to live with his father, a jazz musician, in New Orleans,
and together they survive the horrors of Hurricane Katrina in the Superdome, learning about
each other and growing closer through their painful experiences.
ISBN 978-0-670-06160-0 (hardcover)
[1. Fathers and sons—Fiction. 2. Hurricane Katrina, 2005—Fiction. 3. Jazz—Fiction.] I. Title.
PZ7.V8877Hu 2008
[Fic]—dc22
2007038215

Printed in U.S.A.   Set in Chaparral MM

Special thanks to Joy Peskin, Regina Hayes,
Rosemary Stimola, Jim Cocoros, Catherine Frank.
Extra special thanks to my loving wife, April, who always
had a ready ear during the writing of this story.

—P.V.

• • • • • •

This text is dedicated to those
who lost so much in this tragedy
and who are bravely rebuilding their lives
in the city of New Orleans.

• • • • • •

· · · · · ·

Somebody screamed and my eyes shot open. Only it was still pitch black, and I couldn't see a thing. The air was so thick it almost smothered me, and my lungs had to fight extra hard for a breath that smelled worse than shit and feet mixed together. Then there were flashlights, and footsteps pounding the concrete stairs one section over, and voices of frightened people running to hide from another gang of thugs. I reached next to me to feel for Pop, and on the other side for my uncle. I stopped trying to figure out how scared I was, or if the empty feeling in my stomach would ever quit. The sweat came down my face, stinging the corners of my mouth. Maybe it was 110 degrees. And when those flashlights disappeared, and everything went dark again, it was like somebody shut the oven door on us. My back was stiff and straight in that fold-down seat, and my legs had gone numb hanging over the row in front of me. A plastic garbage bag with everything I had inside was stuffed under my neck for a pillow. I thought about what Pop said when we first got to the

Superdome: *"Don't matter what you see or who needs what—they're not family. It's three of us and nobody else. And that's all it can be."* The wind and rain had beat down on that dome like it was a giant drum. But now, people were pounding at each other. There was a buzzing, and I guess the generators tried to kick back in. The rings of lights circling the stadium started to glow a little. They reminded me of halos over the heads of angels. Then I heard a baby cry with a shriek that nearly stopped my heart cold. And for the life of me, I didn't know if that baby was being born or dying.

Oh, when the saints go marching in
Oh, when the saints go marching in
Lord, how I want to be in that number
When the saints go marching in

Sunday August 28, 7:15 A.M.

Late last night, after Pop finished his gig, he told me to collect up all the things I couldn't live without. He said that we were driving to a motel in Baton Rouge the next morning with Uncle Roy in his old Chevy because of Katrina—a monster hurricane that was coming.

"And Miles, call your mother. I want her to know you're okay, case the phone lines get knocked out," Pop said. "I'm not gettin' cussed at 'cause she's worried sick over where you are."

I'd been with Pop in New Orleans maybe two months, since just after school let out. I'd spent summers with Pop before, but this time it was different—

I was staying for good. Mom had got remarried to a mailman with three kids of his own back in Chicago, and living in that two-bedroom apartment with them all was like being stuck on the Lake Street El train without a seat at rush hour.

"It's hard for everybody in this house. You think you're the only one that's got to change?" Mom would bust on me whenever I complained about it. "You're still my baby, Miles, but I got four children to look after now."

My parents split up before I could remember them ever being together. So I really only knew Pop from the times he'd come around our way to play jazz festivals. But once I turned twelve, Mom said I was grown enough to ride the train to New Orleans myself and spend summer vacations with him. Pop played trumpet at the different clubs with my uncle on slide trombone. I didn't give a shit about jazz. Neither did any kid I ever knew. But once I learned to stomach all that crap about what music meant to his soul, and got past the feeling that I didn't exist to him when that damn horn was in his hands, every night around Pop was like New Year's Eve.

"You think it's gonna be a party livin' with your father year-round. It's not," Mom warned me. "Maybe it's all good in summertime 'cause there's no school. But you're about to be a sophomore in high school and don't put near enough into your grades now—everything's football and horseplay. Somebody's gotta see that you study and make something of yourself. He's not gonna put you ahead of his music. You'll be second-linin' it with him, just like I did. That's where you march *be-hind* the band in the parade. Only your father's so into his playing, he won't even notice when you're not there anymore."

I love Mom, and knew she'd been through plenty of problems with Pop, like his drinking and staying out all night. But he'd always kept a tight lid on that when I was there. It was only his music I had to deal with. She didn't think he'd even want me, and I stressed over hearing that, too. So I was surprised when Pop didn't argue to death against it. Only before I came to live with him for real, he explained to me how it was going to be.

"This house ain't some quiet library to study in. I practice my chops when I need to, and I play on the weekends. When Mardi Gras comes, it's gigs every night, so you gotta look after yourself then," said Pop. "I don't care nothing 'bout Nintendo, basketball, or gangsta rap—even if you do. I live and breathe jazz.

That's it. When I'm blowing free, it's like I'm talkin' to God and he's answerin'—'Doc, you black and strong and beautiful. So play like my angel Gabriel.' And, son, you don't interrupt a man when he's conversing with his maker."

Halfway through that speech, I could feel an earthquake starting in my toes and rumbling up my body inch by inch. I wanted to scream into the phone at Pop that if he ever put his trumpet down he'd know I played football, not basketball. And maybe he'd still have a family instead of a bunch of tourists who clapped when he was finished playing and then went home. But I needed him to come through for me bad. I couldn't stomach Mom's new husband screaming at his kids every two seconds, or never having any private space of my own. So I kept my mouth shut while Pop laid out his rules, and bit it all back.

"Yeah, Pop," I answered. "Any way you want it."

Before I left, Mom said, "Maybe the two of you can grow up and learn some responsibility together."

Pop rented a tiny apartment over Pharaohs, one of the clubs where he played regular, and got me a part-time job. His walls were painted pink and purple, and I'd rank on him, calling it "Skittle House." He'd nailed up black-and-white pictures of famous jazz players with old-school nicknames like Satchmo, Dizzy, and Bird.

"That's the Holy Trinity right there, son," Pop said. "All those MC thugs in bandanas screamin' *niggers*, *bitches*, and *hos* put together couldn't spit-shine their shoes."

There was a picture on a tabletop of Pop, too. He was blowing his trumpet with his eyes shut tight. If he ever opened his eyes and took a good look at me, maybe he'd see who I was. That I had my own mind about things and could think and feel for myself. And that what was important to him didn't mean shit to me.

The first week I was there, everything was good. Pop spent lots of time with me, getting me settled in and registered for high school. It was almost like having a full-time father, something I never knew before. But then Pop's gigs started piling up fast, and he forgot all about me.

Sometimes when Pop wasn't around, I'd open the case and stare at his horn. It was all shiny and gold, but I could see the little dents in it. I'd even pick it up to try and feel why Pop loved it so much. But it was always just cold in my hands. I never once saw Pop try to hold a football like that. Then I'd think about chucking his horn down the garbage chute, and seeing Pop's face when he opened the case and it was empty.

Pop's legal name was Terrance Shaw, but everybody called him "Doc" because they said his horn could blow life into anyone, no matter how stiff they were.

"The city morgue called again, Doc," Pop's friends would joke. "They want to know if you could lighten their load by going down and playin' a set."

I'd just pretend to laugh along.

I had a couch in the corner of the front room for my bed. There was a curtain I could pull closed for privacy, and I learned to sleep with that damn jazz pumping up through the floor from Pharaohs. I'd made the freshman football squad at school back in Chicago last year, and was praying I'd make the varsity here.

I love football because it gives you back everything you put in. It's that simple. If you tackle somebody hard enough, they'll never forget it, and they'll always watch over their shoulder for you. And when you got the ball in your hands, nobody takes their eyes off you, not even the dudes playing in the marching band.

I was expecting some new football gear for my birthday, back in the middle of July. Mom sent me a watch in the mail—one with a metal band that yanked the hairs on my wrist every time I put it on.

But when she called, I made a fuss over it anyway.

Pop even asked me what I wanted for a present. I told him cleats and a new football. Then I came home from football practice the morning of my b-day, and there was an African drum sitting on the couch with a card on top of it.

"That for me?" I asked, ready to blow.

"Read the card and find out," answered Pop, with his arms folded in front of him.

I skipped through the whole Hallmark message part and just saw the *with love, your father* at the bottom.

"Thanks, Pop," I said, super sarcastic. "No wonder you play music by ear—you're such a good listener."

And Pop walked off without saying a word, steamed as anything.

We hardly talked to each other for a week, and I couldn't shake the feeling that I got gypped out of a gift.

Then one night, in between doing sets of sit-ups and push-ups, I was resting on the couch with my arm hanging over the drum. I wasn't even thinking about it, when I started tapping on it to the music from downstairs.

That's when Pop poked his head out of the kitchen and said, "You was born in New Orleans and named after Miles Davis—the most kick-ass trumpet player ever. You ought to be able to beat something respectable on that skin. And I don't wanna hear no scientific crap 'bout some genes skipping a generation."

I didn't want to act like an ungrateful brat anymore, especially after Pop let me come live with him. So I eased up on him about the drum.

"It's an all right present, I guess," I said, without any real feeling.

Football tryouts began in early August, with the final cuts coming when school started up in September. Coach had us on the practice field in the mornings by eight A.M., before the sun got too strong. But I was still drenched in sweat after every scrimmage and needed to drink a gallon of Gatorade to put back what I'd lost. Most of the upperclassmen carried more weight than me, and I knew I had to work my ass off just to make second-string and stand on the sidelines. That's what I was worried about most when we climbed into Uncle Roy's Chevy that morning—missing practices, and losing a spot on the team.

We got to the highway and it was bumper to bumper, with cars stretching as far as I could see. Only none of them were moving an inch.

"This must be the highway to heaven, 'cause everybody's trying to get on it at the last minute," said Uncle Roy, shaking his head.

The three lanes on the opposite side, coming into New Orleans, were totally empty.

People had their car doors swung wide open, and were standing around on the divide. Plenty of them took their dogs along, too. They were barking and growling at each other, and the ones outside kept pissing to mark their territory.

I'd never seen a hurricane before, but Pop and his brother had been through lots of them without a scratch. Then Uncle Roy told a story about how he blew his trombone right into the face of one, because it was named after some woman who did him dirty.

"Florence, Florence, blowin' all over town," Uncle Roy sang, drumming on the steering wheel with Pop's voice joining him in the middle. "You're so damn mean, you want my soul to drown."

At first, I thought Pop was being paranoid about leaving. We lived on the second floor, maybe fifteen feet over the street. I didn't know how the water could reach that high. The landlord had already boarded up all the windows, so unless the wind blew the roof off, I figured we'd be safe.

I grew up with that cold winter hawk ripping down the streets in Chicago so hard you had to walk with your back to it. So I didn't scare off easy.

But the news reports said Katrina was the hurricane everybody always feared. That because she was so powerful, and since New Orleans was built below sea level, the whole city could get swallowed up in a flood if the levees on the river ever busted. And even the mayor said people had to evacuate.

Pop packed his horn—that was automatic. But when he grabbed his gig book that listed every place he'd played and was signed by everybody he'd ever jammed with, I knew he was worried about coming back.

And that got me a little nervous.

I stuffed the sixty-four dollars I'd saved from bussing tables at Pharaohs into my pocket. Then I took an old football with the laces ripped, a sheet of practice plays to study on the ride, and my double-sided practice jersey because I'd already seen Coach flip on some dunce who'd lost his.

"Don't tell me you're thinking 'bout leaving that present I bought you behind," Pop said.

So I took the drum just to humor him, and put everything into a black plastic garbage bag with a couple changes of clothes.

Uncle Roy didn't have a wife and kids, or a place of

his own. He was a *playa* to the max, and mostly lived with whatever woman he was fooling with. He brought his horn with him, a zippered clothes bag with his best suits, and enough candy in a big sack on his lap to answer the door with on Halloween. There were M&Ms, Snickers, Baby Ruth, and Three Musketeers bars all mixed together, and in between smoking cigarettes he'd gobble them down.

I tried to snap on my uncle, calling him "Sweet Tooth Shaw."

But he rolled it right back on me.

"My lady friends can call me 'Sweet Tooth.' That's it," Uncle Roy said. "Now if you ever get a girl to look at you twice, I'll let you borrow that name. You don't have to pay me rent for it or nothin'. Till then, I'll call you Doc's Son, and you call me Uncle—or just plain Roy."

Pop nearly split his sides laughing, and I wished I'd never opened my mouth.

We sat in that traffic jam for three long hours and didn't get ahead more than four or five light poles. I had to beg for them to change the radio from the jazz station, and even settled for the news. The weatherman said the real storm was still almost a day off. But the wind was already kicking up fierce, and I could smell the rain coming.

I put away the sheet with the football plays, and my

eyes landed on the round bronze medal pasted up on the dashboard.

Pop turned around and saw me studying it from the backseat.

"It's a St. Christopher medal, Miles," he said. "He looks after travelers. That's the baby Jesus on his shoulders. St. Christopher carried him across a river and thought it would be nothin'. But it felt like he was haulin' the weight of the whole world."

The needle on the temperature gauge started rising up into the red. Then there was smoke from under the hood, and Uncle Roy cursed that piece-of-shit Chevy up and down. He pounded the car horn so the other drivers would give him enough room to pull off to the side. After the engine died out, Pop and me pushed it the rest of the way to the exit ramp and watched my uncle coast down into a row of empty parking spots on the street.

Workers on a big truck were busy hustling the metal garbage cans off corners—before the wind turned them into flying missiles, I guessed.

All morning, the radio said the Superdome was the only safe place for anybody staying behind. We could see the top of it from where we were, and scrapped the motel idea.

"No choice from here, Doc," said Uncle Roy.

"Guess not," Pop came back.

Uncle Roy opened the trunk and looked at all his shoes lined up there in pairs. Since he didn't have a house, that trunk was like a closet to him.

"I just pray no water seeps into here," he said, slamming it back down. "Hang on tight—I'll be back for you, my babies."

Then Roy pulled an empty green duffel bag from under the driver's seat, and him and Pop put their horns at the bottom of it, like they were hiding them. And with the clothes and other things they piled on top, that bag got so heavy I was the only one who could carry it without stopping to rest every minute.

We started walking with all our stuff, and if Pop and Uncle Roy weren't with me, I'd have probably felt like I was running away from home.

The Superdome's huge and takes up four or five blocks easy. It looks like a cross between a concrete flying saucer, all round and smooth, and some kind of nuclear reactor. The New Orleans Saints pro football team plays there. I'd heard that's where the city's championship high-school game gets put on, too. I'd never been inside it before, but I was hoping the first time I set foot in the Superdome I'd be playing for the city title, instead of running from a storm.

Everybody on the streets around us was headed

there, too—young people, old people pushing shopping carts loaded up with their things, and whole families. And except for the faces of the little kids, they all looked stressed over it.

We were still a few blocks away when the rain started. It came down steady from the beginning. Uncle Roy was the only one with an umbrella, and he was walking with it tipped halfway over my head, too. Then the first good gust of wind tore that umbrella inside out.

"Another dead bird," he said, slamming it to the sidewalk.

The wrecked pieces got blown through the street, and I started thinking how the hawk that clipped it might as well be a hungry vulture now.

Pop stopped us on the ramp leading up to the Superdome with the rain rolling down his face and said, "I don't care how big it is or what kind of slick name they give it—it's still a shelter. Son, your uncle and me spent plenty of days when we were young in places like this, and I won't forget 'em. People are uptight over everything. Drama can jump up out of nothin'. Going in here ain't a game. I want you to be respectful of people—of what they have and what they don't have. But don't close your eyes on anybody, either."

"Lord knows, you right on the money about that, Doc," Uncle Roy said, climbing the next step.

2

Oh, when the sky goes dark and gray
Oh, when the sky goes dark and gray
Lord, I want to be in that number
When the sky goes dark and gray

Sunday August 28, 11:00 a.m.

National Guard soldiers in camouflage fatigues stood at the door with their machine guns pointed straight up in the air. They looked us over like we'd crossed the border from another country without any papers. I locked eyes with one of them who had a thick square jaw, and his grip on the gun got tighter.

There was a big sign just inside the Superdome: EVERY ADULT AND CHILD SHOULD BRING ENOUGH FOOD AND WATER TO LAST THREE (3) DAYS. ALL CITY AND STATE LAWS WILL BE STRICTLY ENFORCED.

Taped underneath was a letter signed by the mayor, ordering that the city be evacuated.

My uncle asked, "How we gonna make groceries, Doc?"

"We'll solve it later, or live off all that chocolate you brought," Pop answered.

"And there's no going back and forth!" a soldier hollered after us. "Once you're inside, that's it! Nobody leaves till we get the all-clear signal!"

"I'd rather have cops than those damn weekend soldiers," my uncle said low, turning into the hall.

"What do you mean?" I asked.

"Maybe their real job's working in a gas station, or a bakery. They train at soldiering something like one weekend a month. Then the state gives 'em a gun during big emergencies and says, 'You're in charge now.' But I guarantee, if shit goes down, they'll either run or start shooting out of fear," Pop said, looking at me. "So you just keep clear of 'em, Miles."

We stepped out into the stadium, under the dome, and the noise hit me like a wave. There were people praying out loud, talking and shouting. Little kids were running through the stands, screaming after each other, and babies were crying their heads off. Almost every one of those voices belonged to black people. I saw some doctors, nurses, and soldiers who were white, but nearly everybody coming to get saved was black like me. And that sat like a rock in the pit of my stomach.

Then I saw the football field, and everything

inside me stopped. I just froze there for a second, looking from one end of it to the other. The grass was the brightest green I ever saw. It didn't matter to me that it wasn't real and was just painted that color. It was like finding the present you'd always wanted under the tree on Christmas morning.

"The boy's seen his Holy Ghost in that field," Pop told Uncle Roy.

There were three tiers of seats sandwiched one on top of another, with a ring of lights between the top two levels. A huge scoreboard hung down from the center of the dome, but it was dark. Families were camped out all over the stands, looking like they'd brought along most of what they owned. They had radios, mountains of clothes, dishes, and portable TVs and VCRs with no place to plug them in. There was even a two-foot statue of the Virgin Mary with dirt and roots still clinging to the bottom that somebody probably dug up from their front lawn. And everywhere we looked to settle, people watched us close, like we might steal what they had.

Pop picked out a section next to an Exit sign, and we piled up our things in a corner closed off by a concrete slab and steel rail.

"Those folks down there got it right," my uncle said, pointing to a small part of the football field that wasn't blocked off by metal barriers. "They got blankets spread out to sleep lyin' flat and everything. That's livin' large compared to these stiff seats. There's more open space. Let's move there."

"Can if you want to," said a woman with her arms around two little girls, a few rows in front of us. "But the soldiers already made them move once. They said that's the first place that'll flood if the dome leaks. But some people is hard-headed, and had to go back."

"We're stayin' put then," Pop said, and wouldn't budge on it.

"That's good! We need more men in their right minds 'round here," the woman said. "I don't trust those soldiers, and the wolves might come howlin' at night."

Uncle Roy went over with his sack of candy, and those two girls waited for their mother to say it was all right before they took some.

Then Pop shot him a hard look, like *we'd* be hungry soon.

I looked out at the field, and couldn't hold myself back. So I put on my practice jersey, with the blue side facing out, and promised Pop I'd quit when the first soldier told me to.

"Go 'head," said Pop with a sour look. "There's

probably worse ways to kill time in this place."

Then I grabbed the football and climbed down. I took a deep breath and turned myself sideways, slipping between the barriers. I'd never been on artificial turf before, and it felt like walking on thick carpet laid over concrete.

The first level of stands was already half filled, and I made believe all that noise was people cheering. Something inside me started churning hot, like I really was in that championship game. So I took off full speed with the football tucked inside of one arm, cutting left, then right. The white painted lines flew under my feet, and I high-stepped it the last five yards. When I hit the goal line, I spiked the ball, and it must have bounced ten feet up in the air. I turned around and a bunch of young kids were chasing after me. They dove for the ball, laughing and yelling like it was a sunny day outside in the park.

I split them into two even teams for a game of touch, and played quarterback for both sides. We knelt down in the huddle, and I drew up plays in the fake grass with my finger.

Everything was going smooth till one of them shoved his brother with both hands in the chest for no reason. The kid who got pushed fell backwards, slamming his head on the ground. I heard it hit solid, and was just glad he got back up. Then he ran off crying to find his mom, and the game was finished. I turned my beams on his asshole brother, staring him down. But he wouldn't even look back at me.

"Yo, Miles!" somebody shouted. "You tryin' out for midget league now?"

It was two guys from the varsity squad, Dunham and Cain. Both of them had on their practice jerseys, too, only with the red side showing.

They each gave me a pound, and Dunham said, "That's three of us now. We just got stronger, case we need to take care of our own."

"Team's family," I said, turning my jersey the same way as theirs.

I really only knew those guys from football. They were both going to be seniors and hung out with dudes from their own class. I'd seen them treat most of the underclassmen like shit on the practice field. But they'd never crossed me. So I liked the idea of rolling with them, and maybe getting bumped up two years on the social chain at school.

"We scoped out this whole Superdome already, and we're just goin' to fill our stomachs," said Cain. "How you fixed for food?"

"I saw that sign outside about it. My family's probably gonna faint 'fore three days are up," I answered. "We can definitely use more eats than we have."

"We'll solve that," Dunham said.

So I started off with them. Then I remembered my football and turned back around for it. There were only a couple of kids left on the field. But they were all playing tag, and my ball with the busted laces was gone.

I wanted to find that little punk who'd decked his brother and body-slam *him* to the floor. I knew it had to be him who snatched the ball, and I stood there steaming.

"Let's go, Miles," Dunham said. "Whatcha waitin' on?"

I didn't want to look like a real jerk in front of them, getting jacked by a fifth-grader. So I kept my mouth shut and sucked it up.

In the corridor, soldiers were handing out a cold spaghetti lunch in a cardboard box. The line was super long, and lots of people standing alone looked really pissed off at being stuck next to other folks' crying kids.

It swung halfway around the Superdome, and I couldn't see the front of that line from the end. That's when Dunham and Cain started moving forward, and I followed.

Cain picked out a spot close up on the line, and asked some old guy standing by himself, "You all right on your feet, Gramps?"

"Doin' o-kay," he answered in a cautious voice.

Then Dunham put a huge paw on the old guy's shoulder, like we were his family, and he'd been holding our spot down.

"That's bullshit!" said some man, maybe ten feet behind us. "You don't belong up there!"

Cain shot him the meanest look I'd ever seen, like he'd stomp on that man's throat if he said another word. The man had a couple of little kids with him. Then I saw him look at the three of us together. I guess he decided it wasn't worth it, because after that, he only said stuff under his breath.

That whole rest of the time I waited in line, I didn't know how to feel. I couldn't decide if we'd just run the winning play in a football game and I should give Dunham and Cain high fives, or if we'd acted like asshole bullies. So I just stood there smiling and nodding my head at them, while that tug of war was going on inside me.

By the time I brought the lunch back to Pop and my uncle, I felt two inches tall about what I did and wouldn't even open the box to look inside.

"Where you been since you left that field, Miles?" Pop asked. "I saw you go off with those two boys."

"I got this food the two of you can share," I answered, handing him the box.

"What about you? Ain't hungry?" Uncle Roy asked.

"Had enough already," I said, pulling off the jersey and stuffing it down into my bag.

Some soldiers dragged an old dude with gray Brillo hair back to our section. He was screaming at the top of his lungs, "This ain't Noah's Ark! It's Nigger's Ark! Ain't two of everything, just us niggers in here. Let me out 'fore God sends his mighty flood!"

"Daddy!" yelled the woman with those two little girls. "Stop it! What's wrong with you? You actin' crazy!"

Pop was the first to recognize him.

"That's Cyrus—that fool dishwasher from Pharaohs," said Pop. "Just pretend you don't know him."

After Pop said it, I recognized him, too.

"He's never been sane," said Uncle Roy. "Just our luck to have him near us."

Another man came back with them. He was a preacher with a white collar around his neck, and told Cyrus, "God gave us this place to be safe, brother. Your family needs for you to be strong."

"Listen to your people, old man," snapped one of the soldiers. "We can't chase you off that damn door all day long."

"Please, Miss, you gotta keep a better eye on your father," said a soldier with more patience. "We can't let him outside, and he's gonna get hurt running around out of control."

"I'll watch him good from now on. I promise. He won't cause no more trouble," the woman said, starting to cry.

"Only God got the right to watch me!" said Cyrus, sitting down. "Nobody else!"

Then he closed his eyes and started singing—

Oh, when the saints come marchin' in,
Oh, when the saints come marchin' in,
Lord, I'm gonna be, be, be in that number . . .

His voice went lower and lower, till it got swallowed up by all the noise. The two little girls were shaking, looking at their grandpa like they didn't know who he was.

"Thank you for goin' after him," the woman told the preacher through her tears.

"Sometimes you need to look after your neighbor's house like it was your own," he answered.

The preacher's family was settled in our section, too. He had a wife and three young children of his own. But he moved them a couple rows closer to help keep an eye on the old man.

"See what it is, but don't get caught up in people's problems, Miles," Pop said. "It'll come back on you. I know."

"How would *you* know, Pop?" I asked, like he never cared about anybody but himself.

"For almost a year, my mama, brother, and me bounced between shelters after our father walked out," he answered, sharp. "Everybody in those places was angry and on edge almost all the time. These people in here, they ain't had long to get used to the idea of maybe losing what they have. And when this hurricane really hits, some of them are gonna be more than tight. They'll be ready to snap."

"Our first gig was in the shelter," my uncle said. "We was in junior-high band class together and the teacher give us each a horn to take home."

"*Home?*" Pop said. "We'd hang around the school-yard for an hour after class, till everybody was gone. That way nobody could see where home was."

"We was just learnin' to play and practiced in the shelter's rec room," said Uncle Roy. "Half the people living there wanted to beat us over the head with those horns for the headaches we gave 'em."

I'd heard that all before and wasn't in any mood for a history lesson.

"Yeah, yeah," I said. "And nobody lived happily ever after."

Pop's face turned hard, like he wanted to boot me halfway across the Superdome for disrespecting his family that way.

Then he looked straight in my face and told me part of the story I'd never heard.

"Some woman was hanging wash to dry on the air vents inside the shelter when this lunatic lady living there started screaming how she couldn't breathe because of it. They got to arguin' so bad it was almost funny. I don't know why our mama got in between them. Maybe she was just sick of all the goddamn noise. But the lunatic pulled a kitchen knife on the other one. Only it was our mama who got stabbed by mistake," he said, slow and even. "She didn't die from it, but she lost a lot of blood. Our mama passed away too young—fifty-six was all."

"Amen to that," Uncle Roy said, crossing himself.

"And I *know* that stabbin' cost her some good years," Pop said.

I started thinking how I'd feel to see my own mother get knifed, and how I'd want to tear anybody to pieces who had a part in it.

"That's a sad story," I said.

"No story," Pop came back. "Just the God-awful truth."

3

We are trav'ling in the footsteps
Of those who've gone before
We'll all be reunited on a new
and sunlit shore
When the saints go marching in

Sunday August 28, 4:10 P.M.

There weren't any soldiers at the front of the line for the bathroom. So anybody who could flex enough muscle just pushed their way past. My uncle and me stood in line for almost an hour, with Pop staying back at the seats to eagle-eye our stuff.

"Look at them crumb punks!" Uncle Roy said as a whole posse of thugs shoved through. "That's how they was raised up. It's a reflection on their family—treatin' their own people like dirt! I hope they meet up with some other gang, and they beat the crap outta each other."

I stood there with my bowels ready to bust, thinking about how I'd snuck onto that food line. And that this was some kind of cosmic payback.

"Maybe it'll come back on them even worse," I said, with the cramps shooting through me.

My uncle nodded and said, "It will, if God *or* the devil's got a hand in it."

There was a guy walking up and down the line, talking to people on the low. I thought he was hawking weed, but he wasn't. Instead, he flashed a box of pills, like you'd buy in a drugstore.

"This stuff will bind you up tight," he said. "You won't have to shit for days."

I looked at him like he was crazy. He wanted ten dollars for a single pill, but Uncle Roy traded him a brand-new pack of cigarettes for one.

We finally got inside the bathroom and waved through a thick cloud of smoke. I could smell the weed mixed with cigarettes, and after a minute, my head started spinning. I felt sorry for some little boy whose father had his hand cupped over the kid's nose and mouth.

Uncle Roy kept watch outside the stall while I went in to do my business. Then I did the same for him. Only people had already robbed all the toilet paper. I guess so they'd have it for *themselves* later, or to sell. So I just pulled my pants up, and didn't let myself think about it.

On the way back, I found that guy and bought two of those pills, for Pop and me. I had mostly fives and singles, so it probably looked like I had more money than I did. People saw that roll in my hand and some of them eyed it good. That's when Uncle Roy got up on me close to show we were together, and I put a grill to chill on my face, advertising that I wasn't a herb.

There wasn't a clock you could look at anywhere. But I had on the wristwatch Mom got me. It was a little after five o'clock, and I was trying to get comfortable in one of those stiff seats. I kept thinking about that bastard kid who'd stole my football. Then I took out that damn drum. I spun it around in my hands and wanted to throw a perfect spiral with it from the stands and see it smash into a thousand pieces on the field. But that wasn't going to fix anything. So I pulled back and left the drum sitting on my lap. Then I pounded on it, like I could put my fist straight through the skin stretched across the top.

"Ease up on that!" scolded Pop. "Remember, that's an instrument, not a toy."

I didn't say a word back, and just sank lower into my seat.

When I called Mom about the hurricane last night, it was late and I'd woke her up.

"Your father's bringin' you where? To what motel?" she started in, still half asleep. "You tell your father and uncle to drive you up here to Chicago. I want you where it's safe."

What really ran through my brain was, *Why? So the three of us can sleep in a closet in your crowded-ass house?*

Instead, I answered, "You know nobody can change Pop's mind when he's set on something."

But I missed her, too. And it stung when she gave up on the idea of getting me there so quick.

"Then you just make sure he fills up jugs of water, and take all the food you can find," she told me.

Only we weren't smart enough to do any of that.

Back in Chicago, Mom was probably setting the table for Sunday dinner around now.

My stomach rumbled and I started beating on that drum dreaming of all the things Mom cooked best. I could taste her macaroni and cheese, pork ribs, and meat loaf with mashed potatoes when Pop said, "That noodlin' almost sounds decent, son. You been down to the Crossroads without me knowing?"

"Down to *where*?" I asked.

"The Crossroads—that's where you learn to play

your ax without havin' to sweat over it," Pop said. "The devil shows up and makes you a deal. You trade him your soul and he gives you the power to play. So you got to choose one road over another—the easy one or the rough one that might never get you there."

"I been nowhere near there, Pop," I said fast, losing my patience. "You ever been?"

"I went there one time but the devil never came. Guess I had nothin' to trade. Jazz had already snatched up my soul," said Pop, picking up my drum. "It's the only way I can say what I feel, and I'd be less than nothin' without it."

Then Pop grabbed the drum and used just his fingertips to beat a rhythm off the top of his head. It cut straight through all the noise, like it had something to say just to me. And I wondered how long Pop suffered on the rough road to make a drum talk that way.

The preacher's name was Culver, and at around seven o'clock that night he stood up on his chair and said he was going to hold a service. Lots of people got up to move closer, and Uncle Roy even unzipped his clothes bag to put on a suit jacket.

"I may be a sinner on Saturday night, but I'll show some respect on the Lord's day," said Uncle Roy.

I hadn't been to any kind of service since I started living with Pop. My uncle and him played every Friday and Saturday night. That's when I could get work bussing tables, too. So Sundays were mostly for sleeping late.

Culver was yelling over the noise from the start.

"Know that Katrina's not some kind of punishment," he preached. "That's not God's way. I'll tell you this storm is a test. It's a test of character, and a chance to prove what's really important to you in this life— faith, family, and the brotherhood we all share."

I could tell parts of that speech were written out beforehand. But sometimes Preacher Culver would go off sideways to answer somebody's question, like, *Why does God have it in for poor people?* He'd pull words right out of the air to come up with an answer. And that's when Culver sounded to me like he meant it the most.

Cyrus sat there stone quiet with his eyes fixed on something in front of him. Then close to the end of Culver's sermon he hollered out, "How 'bout some singin', preacher? It's not a service without a hymn!"

Culver called up two of his own kids who had tambourines. He looked at me and asked, "Young brother, can you come up here with that drum, please?"

I don't know what happened. But I was on my feet

before I knew it, like I never really had a choice.

Then Preacher Culver asked if anybody else had an instrument they could play. Only Pop and Uncle Roy stayed blank on him and never moved a muscle. When I got up front, I stood there looking at them. They both had big grins on their faces, like the joke was on me.

"Just a simple beat," Culver said.

I didn't have the time to think about how I didn't really know what I was doing.

Preacher Culver's hand rose up and down, and I banged on the drum to it, before he started singing alone.

Amazing Grace, how sweet the sound,
That saved a wretch like me . . .

Most everybody in our section joined in, and there were voices coming from other directions, too. And for a minute, the loudest sound in the Superdome came from that song, and everything else faded out behind it.

I didn't sing a word and just concentrated on following Culver's rhythm, trying not to screw up.

When it was finished and I walked back, Pop and my uncle were both clapping for me.

"See, now your first gig was in a shelter, too," said

Uncle Roy, smirking. "Your trio was tight. I didn't hear a single clam in that whole piece. Maybe all you need is the right nickname to crash the big-time. How about 'Chic' for all them years you spent in Chicago?"

"That'll hype him good," laughed Pop. "Two generations of Shaws—Doc, Chic, and just plain Roy, bringing down the house."

I couldn't figure why, but on the inside, every part of me was tingling. I felt like I'd made it past something. It wasn't anything corny, like that Crossroads story Pop told me. But it felt like something I could never lose, even if Katrina did us all dirty and blew everything else away.

Late that night, I was sound asleep in a straight-back seat when my stomach woke me. My eyes focused slow, and I saw the empty football field. At first, I thought it was some kind of dream. That's when the sound of a baby crying jumped between my ears, and every second of being stuck inside the Superdome came roaring back.

"If you're gonna stay up, I'll grab a little shut-eye," Pop said, sitting two seats away.

"Sure, Pop," I said, rubbing the crust from my eyes.

Uncle Roy was sitting with Cyrus's daughter. They

were both smoking cigarettes on the sly after a soldier made them stop before. And my uncle was puffing smoke rings for one of her little girls who was still awake. I thought those two girls had been taking turns holding a teddy bear. Only this time I saw it move in her arms and knew it was a guinea pig. They must have snuck it in, because when we first got here, I saw those soldiers turn away a lady with a dog that small.

More and more people were filling up the stands. New families were scouting around for someplace to settle. It must have been raining buckets outside now because every one of them and their things were soaked ten times worse than when we first got to the Superdome.

Dunham and Cain came walking through the corridor, and I sank down low into my chair. But they spotted me anyway and started waving their arms for me to climb the stairs to where they were. So I turned my back on our stuff.

I reached the top step and saw they had two other guys with them I didn't recognize. Those guys weren't on the football squad, but they were wearing red shirts, too.

"This where you been holed up?" Dunham said. "Damn! We coulda used you, Miles. We had a stare-down with some other dudes over who owned a whole section of people. They had us outnumbered five to four, so we had to blink."

"Forget that shit. Niggers was poor in those seats anyway—welfare cases, straight up," said Cain. "Miles, what do people got in them bags where you are? You see anything with dollar signs on it?"

"Nothing like that," I answered. "It's mostly old folks, women, and little kids. There's even a preacher and his family."

Then somebody saw the candy machine in the corner. Cain watched for soldiers, and a huge heavy dude, who was big enough to play the whole offensive line on a football team by himself, pulled out a switchblade and pried open the coin slot. There was a flood of silver on the floor, and they were all stuffing their pockets with change.

"Get the candy, too!" hollered Cain, kicking in the glass. "Get it all! We can sell that shit for some real dough!"

Dunham came back to me and said, "Go tell that preacher to take up a collection for us. That we'll be his protection from any thugs on the loose. But people gotta pay up first."

"I can't," I told him. "My family's down there."

"That's why you should do it," said the dude with the knife, in a thick bass voice. "You wanna see them safe, right?"

"Come on, Miles. People are scared to death in this joint," Dunham said. "Even if everybody where you are coughs up a dollar—that's fifty, sixty bucks, easy."

When Cain saw I wasn't going for it, he tugged at his red jersey and said, "No wonder he ain't wearin' his colors. This ain't no charity, Miles. This is business. If you ain't down with us, you're against us."

Their eyes all zeroed in behind me, and I spun back around.

"What's the problem, son?" Pop asked, with my uncle coming up behind him.

"No problem, Pop," I said. "Just talkin' to some teammates."

Pop and Uncle Roy got next to me, and those dudes circled around us like a pack of wolves.

That's when Preacher Culver came charging up the stairs, and suddenly the numbers got evened off.

"I don't know what this is all about, boys, but I'm not walkin' away," said Culver, with some real fire to his voice.

I thought about the knife that dude had, and Pop's story about his mama. So I took out my money. Then

I counted out half and stood up in Cain's face.

"Here's what I owe for that jersey I *lost*," I told him, and buried the rest in my pocket.

"Just so you know, you can't never get another one," Cain said, ripping the cash out of my hand. "You off *my* squad forever."

Then I watched them all bounce down the corridor.

4

And when the sun refuse to shine
Yes, the sun refuse to shine
Lord, I want to be in that number
When the saints go marching in

Monday August 29, 6:30 A.M.

Early Monday morning, Katrina hit for real, and nobody needed a weatherman to know it. The Superdome started shaking, like Katrina was slapping its sides with a giant open hand, over and over. And the only time it stopped was when she pulled back to wind up and smack us all upside the head again.

The wind and rain beat down on top of the dome, and I could feel its rhythm. It was louder than the noise from the thousands of people packed inside put together. In my head, I pictured God beating his own African drum, saying, *"Here's my hurricane song."* And you couldn't leave or close your ears to His playing. You had to stay put and listen, till He decided that He was done.

The lights went dead, and everything turned pitch black. For a few seconds, the voices dropped down to a whisper. Then people started shouting, *"Lord! God! Jesus!"*

But He wasn't close to being finished, and the Superdome kept getting rocked.

That's when Cyrus lost it.

"Slave ship!" His voice split the darkness. "It's our Middle Passage to hell! Turn me free! Lord, let me free!"

His daughter screamed for him to stop.

My legs shot up, like I needed to run over there. But I felt Pop's hand on my shoulder, pushing me back down. My heart was running wild. Only I couldn't see a place in front of me for it to go. So it kept pumping overtime inside my chest, till it ran down on its own and started beating slower. Then the ring of lights over our heads began to glow again.

Uncle Roy and Preacher Culver were already with Cyrus. His daughter was standing over him, and one of the little girls had her arms wrapped tight around his legs. I stood up slow and walked past Pop, down to where they all were.

It was warm as anything, but Cyrus was shivering. He looked up from his seat and said, "I know I ain't never getting off this slave ship alive. This is it. I can't just sit and wait. I gotta get out now, or I ain't never gonna see the sun again."

The other little girl was sitting alone, rocking the brown guinea pig in her arms. I bent down low and scratched under its neck. Then she asked if I wanted to hold it, and I said sure. When she took it off her chest to give to me, I saw the rainbow painted across her shirt.

The sound inside the Superdome had changed. There was a hum missing from underneath all that noise. The air was already getting thick and harder to breathe, and I figured out the AC hadn't come back on with the lights.

The Superdome took another solid hit of wind, and a section of the roof ripped right off. You could hear the rivets pop and the metal tear. Everybody was staring straight up. The hole was maybe ten feet wide, and the sky behind it was black as tar. Then a second piece, just as big, flew off.

"I coulda stayed home and watched my own roof blow away!" screamed some woman, raising her fist to the sky.

Then the rain started falling inside on the football field, making a puddle on the artificial turf. Some people ran down to the field with plastic bags, so they could catch the water, to wash with or drink. They were pushing and shoving for the best spots, till a fight broke out.

There was a line for bottled water that Pop and me waited on. The soldiers sat there with their machine guns in front of big wooden skids, with cases of it piled high on top. And if I had just walked in from all that rain outside with the rest of those people who were still filling the Superdome, I would never have believed it. I would have thought for sure those soldiers were guarding gold, or anything but water.

"Two nine-ounce bottles a day per person," a black soldier said. "That's it. Don't come back with a sad story looking for more 'cause it ain't gonna happen."

A man wearing a soaked tank top shouted at the soldier, "Brother, is that all *you* get to drink? 'Cause that canteen hangin' on your belt looks like it holds a lot more!"

"Hell, yeah, they drink more—and eat good, too!" yelled a dark-skinned woman, with the sweat glistening on her cheeks. "They think they're better than us 'cause they got those guns! But those ain't the only guns in here!"

"Again," the soldier started up, "refugees will be provided with—"

That's when that same woman cut him off, screaming, "We ain't no damn *refugees*! This is our country, or at least it's supposed to be!"

Everybody in line backed her up on it and started barking at that soldier, too.

Pop was right. People were more than uptight. I could hear in their voices how every worry inside them was ready to bust loose. And it didn't make me feel any better to know the dude holding the machine gun could have been pumping gas last week and wasn't even a real soldier.

We'd swallowed those drugstore pills and didn't have to shit, but we still needed to piss. And after we got our water and drank it, Pop and me headed for a bathroom. I was shocked at how short the line was. Only the closer we got to the door, the more I understood why.

"Goddamn," Pop said, cupping both hands over his nose and mouth.

It smelled like your head was buried in the toilet bowl, and we weren't even inside yet. A man ran out, holding his breath, with his cheeks looking ready to explode. Then he opened his mouth wide for a gulp of air and said, "There ain't any running water. You can't flush or nothing. The toilets are all backed up over the top."

We got to the door and that smell socked me hard in the gut. I felt the vomit shoot up into my throat and choked it back down. I put one foot inside and saw the used crack vials in a yellow pool of piss on the floor. But I couldn't go in any farther. My stomach wasn't strong enough for it, and neither was Pop's.

The stink followed us everywhere, and you could smell it creeping up on the whole Superdome. Pop and me passed a side staircase, leading down to the lobby. There was a wet patch at the base of the wall where people had already pissed. So Pop undid his pants quick.

"This is how it's gotta be, like we're animals," he said.

Pop stood facing the wall with both hands on his crotch when a woman walked over with a boy in diapers. She pulled the diaper off and shook the loose shit down the stairs. The boy's eyes were opened wide, staring straight at me. The woman wiped his behind and cleaned his diaper with a napkin—all with Pop pissing five feet from them. Then she put the used diaper back on the boy and pulled him away by the hand. Only his head was turned back around to me, with his eyes glued to mine. I waited till they got out of sight. Then I took Pop's place at the wall.

• • • • • •

We got back to our section, and Uncle Roy was sitting with some older guy who'd moved his stuff in with ours.

"Fess!" Pop called out, throwing both arms around him.

The guy was drenched to the bone. Even the blanket he was wrapped up in was dripping. And when Pop finally turned him loose, there was a big wet cross going down Pop's chest and stretching through his arms.

"This is my son, Miles," Pop said, and I shook the guy's cold hand.

"Miles—that's a strong name," he said back.

The man had a bruise under his right eye and looked like he'd had half the stuffing knocked out of him.

"Son, this is Lonnie Easterly—the sweetest clarinet player anywhere. Cats call him 'Professor' out of respect. But we're closer than that, and to me and your uncle he's just Fess."

"You been in a fight, mister?" I asked.

"We all got our asses kicked today by that bitch Katrina," he answered. "I ain't no different. I just hung on longer than most and wouldn't leave my place, 'cause I'm stubborn as a mule. Then the floodwater rose up so high, I had to chop a hole in the roof for the Coast Guard to come and take me out."

That's when Pop and me saw the tears in Uncle Roy's eyes.

"So how bad is it?" Pop said real serious, like he was asking after somebody in the hospital on life support.

I guess Uncle Roy already had the news because he dropped his head and turned away.

"Parts of this city are gone, Doc—blown to hell," Fess said. "It's hit-or-miss. Some of the clubs are still standin', and others look like piles of matchsticks. Either way, we lost plenty. I don't know where we're gonna play our gigs, or who's gonna be there to listen anymore."

Pop looked like he'd been stabbed in the heart. His legs folded underneath him and he slid down into a seat.

I didn't know why, but it hit me hard, too. Maybe it was from seeing Pop so shook. But I felt like something got robbed from deep inside me. Only it wasn't something you could replace so easy, like a stolen football.

Fess grabbed a bottle of brown whisky from his bag. He took a quick swallow and passed it over to Pop.

"That damn she-wolf," said Uncle Roy. "A lifetime of roots tore up in two days."

Pop tilted the bottle all the way back, and I watched

a lot of the whisky disappear. Then he pulled his gig book out of his pocket and turned slow through the yellowed pages of every place he'd ever played. He had the bottle tucked upright inside his arm, and I felt better when my uncle reached over and took it from him.

"Come on, Doc. Save some of this for the good times to come," Uncle Roy said, taking small swig.

I stood right behind Pop, looking at the book over his shoulder. Only every page was the same to me. It was just a bunch of dates at the top, with chicken scratch for writing underneath. But I could see Pop running over every line in his head as if he knew it all by heart.

When Pop finally closed his gig book, he held it tight against his chest. I couldn't remember the last time Pop had hugged *me*, and it started eating at me good. As bad as I felt for Pop, I wondered how far behind his music I really was.

5

And when this earthly weight's too much to bear
Yes, when this weight's too much to bear
Lord, how I want to be in that number
When the saints go marching in

Monday August 29, 12:16 P.M.

A single shot rang out, and a voice screamed right on top of it. Then the whole Superdome got stone quiet, except for the sound of people reaching to pull their kids and family in close. Pop looked at me, and I looked back at him. It wasn't a big space between us, but it felt like it was from one end of a football field to the other.

There weren't any more shots, and after a few minutes, people went back to what they were doing before. But I kept thinking about that space between Pop and me.

It didn't matter that it was after noon, the sky behind the holes in the dome was still pitch black.

Katrina kept slapping at us, and the air was getting hotter and thicker with the smell of shit.

Pop, Uncle Roy, and Fess finished off the whisky, with Pop having more than his share. Then Fess pulled a small flask of gin from his pants pocket, and they started drinking that, too.

Other folks were talking, arguing, praying, and moving back and forth all around them, but those three had their eyes and ears on each other, like they were jamming onstage together.

"One year, when the basketball team played here—the New Orleans Jazz—I got paid to play in these stands with a Dixieland band," said Fess, taking his clarinet out of its case.

"They moved that team to Utah and kept the name," Uncle Roy said.

Then Pop broke out laughing in a voice twice as loud as I was used to hearing him. "The Utah Jazz—can you imagine that crap? What are there, twenty black folks in all of Utah? I'll bet half of them are on that team!"

"Maybe we can go *there* to play, till they put this jigsaw puzzle here back together," mocked Fess.

"The Superdome's beat up, but it's still standing," I said. "Maybe you can play during halftime at a Saints game."

The three of them just stared at me.

"Here's to my son," cracked Pop, raising the flask to make a pretend toast. "Everything's football to him—the rest is all invisible."

That felt the same as if Pop had slapped my face in front of everybody.

I knew he was half drunk, so I tried to forget it. But I was already bruised up on the inside.

"Miles," my uncle said in a quiet voice, "there probably won't be enough people livin' here to go to football games."

"You see that Saints football helmet painted on the field, Miles?" said Fess. "That flower symbol on the helmet's a fleur de lis. The French Kings adopted that as their sign, but it really comes outta the Bible. It's a flower that sprung up from the tears of Eve when God kicked her and Adam out of paradise."

"And that's what's happenin' now, son," said Pop. "God's kickin' us out of *our* paradise."

"Maybe I ain't leavin'," said Fess, raising his clarinet to his lips.

"You sure you wanna blow that here?" asked Uncle Roy. "When some of these animals start grabbing for what ain't theirs, they're gonna remember it."

"And pass up on one last gig in *N'awlins*? *Shiiiitt*. In

a house this big?" Fess came back, before he started to play.

Preacher Culver was walking Cyrus around the stands, I guess trying to get him tired enough to stay put. But Cyrus made a quick turn and headed straight for us.

"Listen to that licorice whip," said Cyrus, snapping his fingers to Fess's playing.

Then he stared at the flask till Pop passed it over to him.

"I know who all of you are. And you the boy that brings me dirty dishes on Friday and Saturday night," said Cyrus, taking a sip. "You all think I'm a fool, but I'm not. I tell the truth and—"

"How 'bout you, preacher?" Pop asked, cutting off Cyrus cold. "You too holy for a drink?"

"Never have been, but this isn't the time for it," answered Culver.

That's when a group of soldiers invaded our section. They were all wearing white masks, like doctors, and you'd think we had some kind of disease they could catch.

"Every one of you, put your hands on the backs of those seats," barked the one with the captain's bars on his shoulders. "We're authorized to search for weapons, and that's what we're gonna do—the women, kids, everybody."

The nameplate over the captain's heart read HAN-COCK, and I could see the outline of his face snarling beneath that mask.

The soldier with the sergeant's stripes on his sleeve was named Scobie, and he came around to the front of us, pulling his own mask down to talk.

"I'm sorry, but we have to search your bags, too," he said, nodding to the other soldiers, who started going through our stuff.

"Stand straight for me," Hancock said, patting down Pop himself. "You smell like a damn drunk."

That hit me harder than what Pop had said. I was burning inside and wanted to tackle Hancock on the spot. But I didn't want to get arrested, and I didn't trust that he wouldn't start shooting. Then Hancock slid over behind me, and ran his hands up and down my sides. I looked over my shoulder to eye that bastard good, when I saw Cyrus sneaking off with the flask. He got all the way up the stairs before anybody noticed. One of the soldiers screamed, *"Halt!"* but Cyrus started running like the devil was chasing him.

Cyrus's daughter tried to run after him, but a soldier grabbed her, twisting her arm back. That's when Sergeant Scobie stepped in, turning her loose.

"Watch my kids!" she yelled to the preacher's wife. Then she took off after her father, cursing the soldiers.

"I'll help bring him back," said Culver.

But Captain Hancock wouldn't let him move.

"You keep your hands on that chair. That collar you're wearin' don't hold any weight with me," said Hancock, pointing to the bars on his uniform. "We'll catch up to the old man. There's no way outta here."

Another soldier found Uncle Roy's sack of candy and gave it over to Hancock.

"That's mine," said Uncle Roy. "That's all our food."

"Yeah? You smash up that candy machine in the corridor to get all this?" Hancock asked, like he already knew for sure.

"I don't need to steal," answered Uncle Roy. "I'm a musician, man."

Then the soldiers pulled out the cases for Pop's and Uncle Roy's horns.

"Open those," Hancock told the soldiers. "I want to see inside."

They unbuckled the black cases and the two gold horns sat there shining inside the red velvet linings.

"Maybe machine guns were gonna be in those

cases," snapped Fess. "Like we was Al Capone and his gang."

"There's nothing else here, sir," Scobie told Hancock.

"Trick or treat," said Hancock, shoving the sack of candy into Uncle Roy's chest for him to take.

As the soldiers left, Pop picked up his horn. His face turned angrier than I'd ever seen it. Then he ripped off a melody that sliced through the stinking air like a rampaging angel on wings. I knew it was just for Hancock to hear—to say, *"I ain't no drunk!"*

To me, every one of those notes felt like a punch to Hancock's head. And right then, I wanted to hear Pop play more than anything—fierce and hard.

The sweat was pouring down Pop's face. When he was finished, I put my hand on his shoulder just to feel what it was inside him, and it was like another hurricane blowing in there.

An hour later, Cyrus's daughter came back exhausted and said she couldn't find her father anywhere. Uncle Roy went over to calm her down. And everybody knew Cyrus probably didn't need any whisky in him to think about climbing through those holes in the top of the dome. If he could ever find a way up there.

Waves of new people kept coming in, and it wouldn't

stop. Only they were looking much worse, and it was like they got rescued from one nightmare to get dropped off in the middle of another.

There was a big fat woman, who couldn't fit in a chair, lying flat on the floor. She was gasping for air, and the man sitting next to her face was moving his hand like a fan to get her more.

A guy in the corridor was doubled over, coughing up blood. His family finally found a doctor in a white hospital coat to help him. But there wasn't anywhere close to the number of doctors people needed.

A woman even heard Pop get called "Doc" by Uncle Roy and Fess, and stopped to ask if he really was one.

"Findin' a doctor's like playing *hide and go seek* in this joint," she said frustrated, tightening the bloody T-shirt tied around her cut forearm. "But it ain't no kids' game. It's for real."

Preacher Culver cleaned up the glass from the candy machine, and that part of the hall got turned into a clinic. There was an old woman in a wheelchair there who never opened her eyes once. I watched a nurse hang a clear bag over the sign with our section number—32H. Then she ran an IV from it into the woman's arm. And if her eyes ever popped open, I figured she would have thought she'd died and got sent to hell.

People were saying the mayor had come through, and saw how bad we had it inside the Superdome. They said he was so pissed off that he started to shake with anger.

"He was cursing, saying how he'd make a phone call to the president who's on vacation and get us help here quick," I heard a man sitting on a laundry bag tell somebody.

I didn't even know the mayor's name. All I knew about him was that he was a black dude. So I couldn't see the president of the whole United States jumping too fast to answer his call.

Cyrus's daughter and Uncle Roy had their eyes glued to the stands, looking for the old man. Every little while, one of them would take a walk, trying to find him, but they came back without him every time.

I was playing the "slap game" with Cyrus's grand-daughters. They took turns putting both hands out, palms-up in front of me, while the other minded the guinea pig. Then I'd lay my hands flat on top of theirs, and they'd try to smack me before I could pull my hands away. They'd laugh hysterically every time one of them would whack me, and I'd shake my hand in the air, like it stung so much I couldn't stand it.

Pop had sobered up, and came over to do the "bull-frog" for those girls.

"That baby weasel you're holdin' don't eat frogs, does he?" asked Pop, making his voice deep. "'Cause I'm part bullfrog."

"He's just a guinea pig. He can't hurt you," answered the one with the rainbow on her shirt.

So Pop put a finger over his lips to keep them closed. Then he puffed his cheeks and neck up with air, like when he blew his horn. His cheeks got so big you'd think they were going to burst. The two girls laughed like crazy, falling over each other.

That face was one of the first memories I had of Pop growing up. He'd probably made it for me staring down into my crib.

Then I thought about the times I missed out on with Pop when I was younger. And I wondered what kind of times we were going to share from here on, especially if we didn't have anyplace left to live.

That's when I heard Cyrus yelling from somewhere. I knew it was him because his daughter's head was on a swivel, too, looking all around. He was screaming wild about something, and his voice got higher and higher. Then I heard lots of people gasp all at once, like when something terrible is about to happen on a movie screen.

There were shrieks, and I saw Cyrus fly from the top tier. He'd jumped. His body rocketed through the air, like he was shot straight down out of a cannon.

"God, no!" his daughter cried out, turning away from the field.

Both little girls were facing me and didn't see it. So I let my hands drop quick onto the palms of the one who was holding them out flat. I heard Cyrus's body crash onto the concrete floor under the football field. It was a sickening sound, like a bag of bones hitting the face of a sledgehammer.

I stood there frozen, and felt his granddaughter smack my hands, again and again.

6

Oh, when that rhythm starts to go
Oh, when that rhythm starts to go
Lord, how I want to be in that number
When the saints go marching in

Monday August 29, 5:45 P.M.

None of us went running down to the football field.
We just stayed put. We already knew there was no way
Cyrus could have survived. His body was lying facedown on an empty part of the football field, with folks
starting to gather around him.

Cyrus's daughter collapsed to her knees, pounding
the concrete steps with both fists.

"Why? Lord, why did we have to be here? Why?" she
cried out in a tortured voice. *"I need my babies! Lord,
where are my two babies?"*

Her little girls, who still didn't know what happened, ran into her arms. And their mother hugged
them so tight she nearly squeezed the life out of them.

Pop came over and stood as close to me as he could. I would have given anything to have Pop hug me like that. But I knew we had too many things in the way.

"Why'd it have to happen like this?" I asked.

"I don't know," Pop answered. "It just did."

After a while, Sergeant Scobie showed up and said how bad he felt, but that somebody had to identify Cyrus's body, because they found no ID on him. Then I heard him tell Preacher Culver on the low, "It's not a pretty sight to see."

Cyrus's daughter was too broken up to do it. Uncle Roy said he'd go, and so did Culver. I was shocked when Pop told my uncle to stay behind with Cyrus's daughter—that he'd go with Culver instead. Pop had talked hard against getting involved with anybody else's problems. But he'd just crossed his own line.

Sergeant Scobie gave Cyrus's daughter a paper and pen, and she took her arms from around her kids just long enough to write out her father's full name and birthday. Then Pop and the preacher followed after Scobie, and I fell right in behind them. Pop didn't argue about me going along. But he turned to me and asked, "This the first dead man you'll be seeing, son?"

"Except for TV," I said.

"It takes some gettin' used to," said Pop. "Don't be

ashamed to turn your eyes away. You hear me, Miles?"

I nodded my head and could almost feel Pop's arms around me.

And that was all the support I needed right then to keep strong.

Cyrus's body was under a white sheet, and some soldiers were carrying it away on a stretcher. Captain Hancock waved them past a whole platoon with their machine guns out. Then Scobie gave those guards a thumbs-up for us to follow through a big metal door.

It was a giant freezer. We pushed our way through the thick plastic strips hanging down from the ceiling by the door, and it was like walking into another world. It wasn't cold enough to see your breath, but it was probably forty degrees cooler in there, and the stink was gone, too. The air wasn't heavy, either. It flowed in and out of your lungs smooth, and breathing was almost easy.

There were maybe fifty boxes of food stacked up in one corner, and hundreds of empty ones torn open on the floor. The soldiers lined up two of the wooden skids that those boxes had been delivered on, laying the stretcher across them.

"That's right. Keep him off the floor," Hancock told them. "I can't have any rats getting at him."

Then Hancock pulled down his white mask and said, "Who's it gonna be?"

He had a scar across his left cheek that made him look like an evil G.I. Joe.

"I know him the longest," Pop said, stepping forward.

"Did he look close to this?" asked Hancock, pulling back the top half of the sheet.

Cyrus's neck was all crooked, and his shoulder blade was sticking through his black skin.

"Yeah, I still recognize him," said Pop, straight out. "No matter how much of his dignity you try to take."

Pop and Hancock stood there, grilling each other.

"For all those people out there, there's no more food than this?" asked Culver, breaking the silence.

But Hancock never answered that question.

"Is that the deceased's information?" Hancock sneered, snatching the paper from Scobie's hand. "Escort these *evacuees* back to where they belong, Sergeant!"

But before we left, Preacher Culver laid his hand on Cyrus's leg and said a short prayer. And when he was finished, Scobie was the first to say, "Amen."

When we got out of Hancock's earshot, Scobie told us, "Captain's a professional soldier who's seen real time in wars. I don't believe he's too partial to civilian rescue duty."

"How about you?" I asked, without thinking.

"Me? I'm a high-school science teacher from Irving, Texas," he answered. "But I got family in Louisiana and Mississippi that's got to run from this storm, too. So I want you all to be treated the same way I hope somebody's lookin' after them."

"God will be there for 'em, brother," Culver said. "You can trust in that."

As we stepped back out into the stink and the Superdome crowd, I thought about shaking Sergeant Scobie's black hand. But they were both glued to his rifle.

At our seats, Uncle Roy said it might be a long time till Cyrus got any kind of decent burial.

"They can measure him for a wooden coat, but there ain't no dry ground to dig a grave," said Uncle Roy. "I know he was a pain to put up with, but in a way, he was one of our own. He worked at Pharaohs for as long as I can remember—washing dishes underneath you, Doc, while you walked the floor over his head."

"His family's gotta live with him in a freezer?" asked Fess. "That's no way to mourn proper."

Pop stared out at the middle of the football field

where the Saints' helmet, with that flower on the side, was painted. Then he grudgingly said, "Maybe we need to march for him—send him off right, like he deserves."

The three of them agreed, and Uncle Roy went over to talk to Cyrus's daughter and Preacher Culver about it. I'd seen a jazz funeral once before, when I was visiting Pop during summer vacation and one of his musician buddies passed on. A band marched through the street behind the casket. They played music every step of the way, and by the time it was done, you couldn't tell if the people were sad the dude had died or having a party over it.

Cyrus's daughter wanted the march bad for her father.

"It was the music he loved at that club, not washin' those damn dishes," she said. "I want people to know he's gone, and how much his family's gonna miss him."

She tore a cardboard beer ad down from the wall and printed on the back, in big letters with a black marker somebody lent her, CYRUS ODELL CAMPBELL, DECEMBER 24, 1934–AUGUST 29, 2005.

Pop put a serious look on his face. Then him and Roy reached down to the bottom of our duffel bag.

"Everybody's gonna know 'bout these horns now," Pop said.

"I hear ya, Doc," Roy said, solemn.

Cyrus's daughter stood in the corridor, holding the sign out in front of her, with one of her little girls on each side. Preacher Culver was just a step behind her. After that came Pop, Uncle Roy, and Fess lined up three across with their instruments. I knew it wasn't about me, but I felt lost, like I didn't belong anywhere.

"You gonna get that drum and play?" Pop asked me.

I grabbed it and went to stand in line behind them. Then Pop moved over a step, making a space for me right next to him.

"We start off playin' slow and sad, Miles, like Cyrus passing was the most painful thing in the world," Pop explained. "When that's finished, we play with the joy of him going to a better place and never having to suffer again. The slaves who started this in these parts believed when they died their souls went back to Africa. So it's only right that we got your drum."

I looked around the Superdome at all the black faces and remembered Cyrus screaming out how it was another slave ship. Then I forced myself to take a deep breath and stomached the smell.

"Give me a beat, Miles," said Pop. "One . . . two . . . three . . . four."

My hand hit the drum and we all started forward. We headed down the corridor with Pop's trumpet crying out a sad tune. He was playing right on top of my drumming. And after all this time, it finally felt like we were together on something. Then Uncle Roy and Fess joined in.

People all over the stands were watching. I could see in their eyes how much they'd lost, and how they were mourning, too. They were crying real tears, and some of them even started marching behind us.

The sweat was burning my eyes, but I wouldn't stop playing to wipe it away. More and more people got up to march. And just when I felt my heart sink as low as it could go, Pop turned it around with his trumpet. He let loose a string of notes that pulled me up from the bottom. It was time to celebrate, and everything inside me started jumping. Uncle Roy and Fess were right on it, too, and my hand was pounding the drum faster and faster on its own.

"I feel we're headed some place better, Lord!" Preacher Culver called out. "Maybe we're not worthy, but let your music lead us anyway!"

The people behind us were dancing more than

marching now. A woman with an open umbrella jumped into line, pretending the wind from the hurricane was pulling her along. In the stands, people were clapping their hands in rhythm as we passed. And when Pop started playing "When the Saints Come Marching In," plenty of people started singing along.

We'd made one whole lap around the Superdome and were back where we started. The march was over. Cyrus's family and Culver turned down the stairs to their seats. Only we kept on playing in front of our section, till everybody dancing behind us disappeared down the corridor.

Pop looked at me like he'd never been prouder to have me for a son. I felt closer to him, too. But deep down I didn't know how I could trust it. All my life I'd been second-string behind Pop's playing and grew up hating his music. If banging a drum was going to make Pop see me different, maybe it wasn't worth it.

The second we stopped playing, I felt a streak of cold shoot down my spine. I wanted to take off running down that football field till I sprinted out of my skin and into some other family.

"Cyrus woulda appreciated what your drum had to say 'bout him," Pop told me. "Anybody woulda."

I wanted to scream at Pop that I wasn't like him. That I didn't need music to talk for me. The words were spinning through my head, only my tongue couldn't get a good grip on them. Anyway, I didn't want to start arguing with him. Not now. So I hit the drum one time as hard as I could, and walked off.

7

And when the moon turns red with blood
When the moon turns red with blood
Lord, how I want to be in that number
When the moon turns red with blood

Monday August 29, 9:48 P.M.

The later it got, the tighter the stands became packed with people. The lights kept fading lower, and my eyes were constantly trying to adjust. I was just hoping to sleep. The storm outside sounded like it was easing up, and my stomach was howling worse than the wind now. Except for a few candy bars, I hadn't eaten any real food since before we got to the Superdome on Sunday morning.

It was closing in on ten o'clock when a fire broke out two sections over. I smelled the smoke before I saw the flames. Then I opened my mouth, but Pop found his tongue first.

"Fire! Miles, everybody up!" he yelled.

Pop grabbed his horn with one hand, and me with the other.

We all shot to our feet, rushing in different directions, and couldn't get out of each other's way. Everybody between the fire and us was scrambling, too. Most of them were pushing right towards us, climbing over the rows of seats. We got jammed up hard and couldn't move. I felt the weight of them pinning me, till I almost couldn't breathe. It was like fighting to keep my head above water inside of one big black wave.

I'd never been so scared or felt so small.

Uncle Roy slipped down, and I stepped square on his back by accident. That's when I felt that guinea pig go flying past my feet.

Pop had a death grip on my arm and wouldn't let go for anything. But I couldn't tell if he was keeping me up or dragging me down with him. And just when I thought I was going under for sure, that bottleneck busted loose and we finally broke free, spilling out into the aisle.

Two men beat down the flames with the shirts off their backs.

When the fire was out, and everything was safe, Pop pried his fingers loose from my arm. I could feel the bruises raising up where his nails had dug into me.

"You all right?" Pop asked, with his horn still clutched in his other hand.

Before I could answer, Fess, who was holding his ribs on the left side, said, "This Superdome 'bout to kick me senseless, Doc."

So Pop and Uncle Roy helped him back down the steps and left me where I was standing.

A woman in the corridor started screaming "Rat!" as she tried to stomp that guinea pig dead with the heel of her shoe. It jumped back and even showed its teeth. Then I saw it jet past her and streak down the hall, running for its life.

People were whispering that thugs had started the fire, trying to shake folks down. But it had happened too far away to know for sure.

The soldiers never showed up to check on what happened, and after everybody got settled in again, the fire alarm went off.

ERT! . . . *ERT!* . . . *ERT!* . . . *ERT!*

The sound pounded my eardrums. I shoved a finger into each ear, but even that couldn't stop it from getting through. It pierced every nerve I had, till my heartbeat kept the same rhythm as that damn alarm.

People stood at their seats, turning in every direction. They were looking for the fire, ready to run. Only there weren't flames anybody could see, just the smell of the last fire mixed with that sickening stench.

Pop tried to tell me something as loud as he could, but the sound of that alarm swallowed up his voice like it was nothing.

After five minutes, people started sitting back down, trying to think through that deafening sound. But I couldn't.

It kept stabbing at my ears—*ERT! . . . ERT! . . . ERT! . . . ERT!*

When it finally stopped, I swear my heart skipped a beat, waiting for it to kick back in. I sank into my seat, exhausted and beat up, like I'd just been gang-tackled by the whole Chicago Bears football team.

It was just after midnight and into Tuesday morning when the lights died out, and the Superdome went completely dark. People were cursing out loud at anyone they could think of—God, the soldiers, the mayor, their own mother, anybody. All over the stands, people sparked their lighters to see by, and dots of light kept popping up then burning out everywhere.

"Them soldiers should free us from this joint by sunup," said Pop in the glow from Uncle Roy's lighter. "If the levees on the river don't bust, all that water Fess seen in the streets will go down. Some places gotta be left standin'."

"How high was it?" my uncle asked Fess.

"Tall as a man," he answered.

"Some of those shoes I had in my trunk were alligator. Maybe they swam for it." Uncle Roy grinned, turning it into a joke. "You know tickets for these same seats probably went for five thousand dollars the last Super Bowl they had here. Now we got 'em for nothin' to see the Shit and Stink Bowl."

Only nobody laughed at that one.

"I'm gonna play the high-school championship game on this field one day," I said flat out. "I'll get you all free tickets for that."

"I know you will, son," Pop said, looking me in the eye. "There's no doubt."

And hearing that touched me to the core.

Screams echoed through the stands—chilling ones. And even in the dark, I wouldn't close my eyes.

A flashlight beam came swinging down the corridor. I thought maybe it was the soldiers back on patrol, but then I heard Cain's miserable voice.

"Those are ours now—give 'em up!" he barked.

Dunham and those other guys were with him, too,

and they ripped the flashlights away from a doctor and nurse working in the hall behind our section.

Then Cain and one of his thugs came halfway down the stairs, while Dunham and the heavy dude with the knife—the one who'd pried open the candy machine—stood guard at the top.

Cain grabbed some skinny guy sitting alone by the collar.

"You want us to burn your shit?" Cain threatened him as the thug went through his bag.

"Please! Leave me be! Take what you want!" the guy cried.

The helpless sound in that guy's voice pushed me to my feet. Pop and Uncle Roy were up, too.

I almost couldn't believe it. But there they were, ready to fight for some guy we hadn't even noticed before.

Pop and my uncle had come to the Superdome looking to mind their own business and only care about their own. But somewhere over the last two days, that had changed. Maybe it was Cyrus jumping, or seeing every black face here going through the same thing—stressed out over the thought of losing most of what they ever had—that made them all start to look like family.

Cain was five or six rows away from us, with lots of people in between. So we stood there like stone statues that wanted to move but couldn't.

"We'll burn out this whole section if we don't get paid!" Cain screamed.

Preacher Culver was closer and fought his way into the aisle, hollering at Cain to stop.

"You Miles's preacher man," said Cain, shining his light in Culver's eyes. "You got in our way before."

Cain killed his flashlight, right before him and his thug charged at Culver.

I heard the air leave Culver's lungs as they crashed into him, and his head crack open on the cement steps.

Pop, Roy, and me pinballed off each other, trying to get at that bastard in the dark. Then Uncle Roy got out in front of us with his lighter. But Cain was already standing back at the top of the stairs, surrounded by his crew.

"Where is he?" shouted Cain, pointing his flashlight at us, till my face was the only one in it. "We'll be back, Miles! I know you'll take up that collection for us now! Right? Before we smash up those instruments so nobody has to hear that fucked-up music again!"

"People might even pay us more to do that!" cackled Dunham.

Preacher Culver was lying at the bottom of the stairs, and his family was trying to sit him up.

"Don't worry 'bout me," he muttered, with everybody sparking up their lighters around him. "I'll be all right."

Then Culver put his hand to the back of his head, and it was covered in blood—the same red color as Cain's jersey. But he kept on playing it down.

Before Cain and his crew left, Dunham lit some paper on fire. He tossed it on top of somebody's stuff, while that whale with the knife kept people back. The plastic garbage bag and everything inside it went up in flames quick.

"Don't forget who we are!" screamed Cain, heading down the dark corridor.

"Nobody better forget!" Dunham echoed after him.

I watched Pop and my uncle and lots of other people stomp out that fire. Somebody even poured the last of their drinking water on it to make sure it was out.

"Pay them!" Cyrus's daughter cried. "Just pay those damn bastards. What if my babies get burned up? I can't lose no more family here!"

Then she pulled her front pocket inside out and pushed a handful of singles at me through the shadows.

But I never moved for them.

Fess picked up his clarinet and started playing.

"Blow it loud, brother," Pop told him. "Nobody threatens our instruments—not the mother-tongue."

"Hell, no," said Roy. "Not in this lifetime."

I thought about the music I'd made with Pop on Cyrus's march—how it changed from sad to celebrating in just one beat. I remembered my hands moving to that new rhythm, and how I'd almost seen Cyrus's soul sailing over a river in Africa, beneath a clear blue sky and shining sun.

ERT! . . . ERT! . . . ERT! . . . ERT!

Then my hands clenched tight to the sound of that fire alarm starting again, till they were both balled up into fists.

8

Oh, when my brother's lost his way
And his mortal soul has gone astray
Lord, how I want to be in that number
When the saints go marching in

Tuesday August 30, 2:30 A.M.

The screams kept coming and wouldn't let up. The worst ones echoed down from the upper deck, where there were less people, and fewer eyes to witness any crimes. Families from up there were moving down fast, and some of them settled into our section. There weren't any open seats left, so they camped out in the aisles, or on the floor in the corridor.

"They're raping women and children upstairs—there's gangs of them runnin' wild," said a man in a torn shirt with his wife and kids holding on to both his arms. "I heard they tossed a baby off the top deck, too. I didn't see it, but I wouldn't be shocked at nothin' no more."

The heat was stifling and the lights had come on enough to see maybe twenty feet in front of you. I watched close as the doctor stitched up the back of Preacher Culver's scalp without Novocain. And Culver squeezed his wife's hand, wincing in pain.

"You gotta have the kind of faith you can hold on to," Culver told the man who'd escaped the top tier. "God gave you the wisdom to move down here. I know He's watching over this section 'cause we been looking after each other, like He wants all His children to."

"That's what we aim to do when them crooks come back," said Pop, standing at the top step with Uncle Roy and some of the men from our section behind him. "We're gonna look after our own."

"If violence comes to us, I'll stand with you," said Culver.

"Feel your head, preacher," Uncle Roy said, flat. "It's already been here."

"I won't fight out of anger and revenge, brother," he answered. "It's my blood spilled, and *I'm* willin' to let it go."

Then the doctor pulled the needle through the back of Culver's head one last time, before he tied off the thread in a knot.

Half the people didn't want a scrap with Cain and

his crew, and collected up ninety-two bucks to pay them off. Since Cain had called my name out, they wanted me to hand it over.

"I don't like it," Pop said straight out. "But you the one who *knows* them, Miles, and you man enough now to make your own decisions."

It felt good to hear Pop call me a man and at least part recognize I had my own mind.

But before I had to decide, Culver took hold of the money that people collected.

"I won't add a dime to it. I'm not payin' the devil to enjoy God's gifts," he said, putting the money inside a brown paper bag from the floor. "But if this is what some of you want, *I'll* do it. Those boys got a grudge against Miles. I don't trust them."

I wasn't about to argue with a preacher who just took twenty stitches with nothing to numb the pain.

We started to see some soldiers again. Now they were patrolling in bigger groups. They looked twice as tense as before, and were eyeing people like we were in a war zone. Cyrus's daughter had to throw herself in front of a whole squad to get their attention. And when she did, some of them jumped forward, like they might have to beat her down.

"You got to stop these thugs from comin' back and

burning us out!" she screamed at them. "'We need pro-tection!"

"If they were here now, we'd stop 'em. But they're not," the lead soldier said.

"Then leave some of your men behind for when they *do* come," she begged.

"I can't. I gotta follow orders," he said.

She wouldn't move from in front of them.

"It's your job to keep women and children safe!" she hollered.

They ordered her to step aside. And when she didn't, one of the soldiers turned his gun sideways and put it across her chest, shoving her out of the way.

Then the soldiers marched off, with Cyrus's daughter cursing them from behind.

Later, two city cops passed through the hall with their guns drawn. Preacher Culver tried to call them over to our section, but they wouldn't answer him. Then one of the cops bent down low on one knee. He put his hand over his face and began bawling like a baby. The other cop stood over him, looking all around at who might be coming. That's when Culver quit calling.

"With the sufferin' they see every day, even the cops can't take no more of this," Pop said, standing with the other men, guarding our section.

"They're only human," answered Culver. "He might have lost more than we can imagine today."

"I just don't like seeing a man with a gun in that frame of mind—not when he's got a badge to back it up," Uncle Roy told them both.

In all the time we watched for Cain, Fess blew his clarinet. He looked to me like he wasn't strong enough to walk around the block at a good clip. But I guess his lungs were built up better than the rest of him, because he never ran out of breath. I was almost suffocating. Breathing in the Superdome was like having your head under a heavy blanket on the hottest, most humid night you could imagine. Only that didn't slow up Fess any.

"Let the good times roll!" a woman one section over shouted to him.

Still, I could hear in her voice how she was stressed to the max.

I saw a straight-haired girl I recognized in shorts and no shoes, huddled in the corridor with her mother. She was on the cheerleading squad and had been at football practice a few times. I'd talked to her once but couldn't remember her name. I wanted to feel something different instead of all this pressure, so I went over. I hadn't brushed my teeth in a couple of days and knew my breath was kicking. But I figured it couldn't be any worse than the stink in the Superdome.

"Pardon me. I'm Miles," I said. "I met you before at—"

That's when the girl and her mother both freaked out.

"We don't know you! Keep away from us!" her mother screamed, like I was going to attack them.

I tried to say something back, but the girl looked scared out of her mind, shaking her head at me. I was stunned. Then Pop came over and apologized to them.

"Maybe this ain't the best time to make acquaintances, son," he said on the walk back. "People are hardly themselves now."

It was nearly four o'clock in the morning, and the glass on my watch was fogging over from the humidity. The stadium lights had come up a bit brighter, and I noticed a pair of birds that got inside beating their wings against the top of the dome. They flew in circles, till I almost got dizzy watching them. Then one found a hole in the roof, and the other followed him out. Only a minute later, they were both back inside, searching for a way out again.

There was yelling from down the hall and footsteps

flying our way. Everybody who was ready to fight filled the aisle. Fess even stopped his playing. That's when a different gang of thugs—one in orange bandanas—came running out of the shadows. People in our section grilled them hard, and I felt my blood pumping as fast as their feet. But they weren't interested in us. They streaked right past our section, running from something.

"There's the devil you know, and the devil you don't know," said Uncle Roy, watching them go.

I asked which one was worse, and he answered, "Whichever one got the other haulin' ass like that."

A few minutes later, Cain and his crew came down the corridor. I saw right away that they were one body short. Dunham was missing, and Cain's hands had cuts and were stained with blood.

Pop and Uncle Roy had me sandwiched between them, and Fess held his clarinet tight inside of one hand, like it was a wooden stake he might have to drive through some vampire's heart.

"Where's my do-re-mi, Miles? Remember who owns these seats right here—me!" Cain said, pointing to himself. "Nobody else!"

Preacher Culver gave the paper bag with the money to Cain, who tossed it over to one of his two boys. The guy counted it fast. Then he nodded at Cain.

"You got what you wanted," Culver said. "Now leave these people to deal with their troubles and grief in peace."

"How 'bout me, preacher? You wish me peace, too?" Cain asked in a sharp voice.

"I do," Culver answered.

"Even after I busted the back of your skull?" said Cain.

"That's right," said Culver, without blinking.

Then Cain spit right into Culver's face and said, "Why don't you turn the other cheek to that, and I'll hock up another load for you."

Culver's eyes turned to fire, like he was staring down the devil. But he didn't budge an inch.

I slipped past Pop and my uncle, pulling out what was left of my own money.

"Miles, come back!" shouted Pop, with his arm grabbing nothing but air.

"I want you to have this," I told Cain, holding out the roll.

But when he reached for it, I slammed my forehead into his face, knocking him flat.

Cain got off the floor screaming at his crew to keep back.

"Leave 'em!" he said, coming at me. "He's mine!"

I wrestled him down, and we were tugging at each other so wild that Cain's shirt got yanked off right over his head. We'd been scrapping for maybe six or seven "Mississippi"s when I heard a stampede of feet thundering towards us. At first, I thought it was Pop and everybody else from our section wanting to kick Cain's ass, too. But it wasn't. It was a whole family of people I'd never seen—something like twenty of them, and every one was thirsty for blood.

Cain's crew split, even the heavy dude with the knife.

Those people tugged Cain and me apart, pinning us down.

"It's one of them two who put his hands on me!" a woman screamed all hysterical.

"Which one?" snorted the giant on top of me, holding Pop back with one arm.

That's when Cain pointed at me and cried, "He did it! That's why I was whippin' his ass! It was him!"

"No! The other one!" the woman hollered. "It was dark, but I'd know his voice anywhere! *That's* him!"

That family grabbed Cain by his arms and legs and nearly ripped him in two. They beat him bloody, kicking him through the corridor.

Cain was screaming at the top of his lungs as they dragged him down the steps to where nobody else could see.

Pop had his arms wrapped tight around my chest. I knew that could have been me in Cain's place, and I felt the blood pulsing hard at my temples.

I wanted to shut out Cain's voice bad, but I couldn't. And the worst part was that it didn't sound like there was any soul inside his screams.

"Only God can save him now," said Preacher Culver.

9

Oh, when the sun begins to shine
Oh, when the sun begins to shine
Lord, how I want to be in that number
When the sun begins to shine

Tuesday August 30, 6:52 A.M.

Katrina had finally run out of steam, and the sunlight poured through the holes in the roof of the Superdome. Then the noise inside rose up louder than it had ever been. People a couple of sections over were grabbing all their things and running into the corridor.

"This is it!" shouted Pop. "They're lettin' us go! Come on, quick—get everything together!"

Almost as soon as he'd said it, there was a squad of soldiers by the exit sign behind our section getting people into a line. Then just as fast, they started sending everyone down the stairs. The Superdome was shaking with footsteps. I picked up the duffel bag with Pop's and Uncle Roy's horns inside, while they took the rest of our stuff and most of Fess's, too.

Cyrus's daughter and her two girls had joined up with Preacher Culver and his family. They were all still getting their things together. Uncle Roy and me looked at each other like maybe we should wait for them. But there was no slowing down Pop.

"Preacher, you keep on with God's work now. You hear?" Uncle Roy called out.

But for the first time, Culver was too busy with his own family to answer.

I saw Cyrus's granddaughters and thought about what Katrina had cost them. I didn't know who they could grow up to blame or sue—the soldiers, the governor, or even the president of the United States. I was thinking how even the Supreme Court wouldn't be high enough. That maybe they'd have a beef directly with God for sending the storm and making their skin the color that didn't get saved fast enough.

Then I looked down at the football field. Even under all the ripped papers, water-soaked cardboard, and piles of garbage, it was still the brightest green I'd ever laid eyes on. But I knew when I finally made it to the city's championship game, that field wouldn't feel the same under my feet as it did the first time. It couldn't—not after everything that happened here.

"Hurry now!" called Pop, ready to leave us behind.

We started down the stairs so close on each other's heels you'd think we were chained together. There was shit smeared across the wall of the first landing. Everybody turned their noses and had to lean hard the other way not to brush up against it.

"If I could walk outta this joint blindfolded I would," said Uncle Roy.

"They oughta knock it down to the ground after what people went through in this place," said Pop, breathing through his mouth.

We hit the big open hall at the bottom and saw the doors the soldiers were pushing people through to the outside.

"Hallelujah!" voices shouted, one after another.

The floor was slippery as ice, covered in soaked ceiling tiles that had come crashing down. People were falling everywhere in front of us. Pop grabbed Fess by the belt so he wouldn't go down, and we practically skated to those doors.

I had both hands on the back of Pop's shoulders when I stepped out of that tomb. The bright sunlight stung my eyes, but I couldn't turn my head from it. Then I swallowed a breath of clean air, and I guess that was as close as you could come to being reborn.

I stopped to feel the sun on my face, and to be

sure that my feet were really on solid ground. Then I focused my eyes and peeped at what Pop had already seen. The soldiers had put up barricades all around the concourse—a flat cement area surrounding the Superdome. They were guarding every exit tight. Nobody was going home. We were just being herded somewhere new. Only this pen was outside in the open. And all the worn-out, beat-down people dragging their stuff started scrambling all over again to find a spot to claim.

"They can't keep us locked up no more," said Pop, defiant. "Not like this."

Then Pop pushed forward till he reached the barriers where Captain Hancock and Sergeant Scobie were stationed with a squad of soldiers. He got right up to the waist-high fence, and was almost face-to-face with them. But Pop never said a word. Instead, his eyes were fixed in the direction of Pharoahs, where we lived. That dark filthy water was everywhere. It was over the roofs of cars in some places, just below the bottom branches of trees, and people were swimming towards the Superdome.

The concourse was way above street level, so we were safe. Opposite us were maybe a hundred people who'd climbed the highway overpass to escape the water, and were trapped now on every side by the flood, yelling and waving for help.

"It's a damn nightmare come true," said Uncle Roy.

Almost all the windows in the big office buildings were blown out. Dark smoke funneled up into the sky from probably a dozen different fires around the city, and a black rainbow stretched across New Orleans.

"No one is allowed to leave this area! We are under an evacuation order," announced Hancock over a bullhorn. "If you do not follow our instructions and remain lawful, you will be subject to arrest. Continue to comply with our orders. Everything we do is for *your* protection."

And that just felt like one more kick in the teeth coming from Hancock's mouth.

We settled in right up against the barriers, just outside the Superdome. The sun was blazing, and there was hardly any shade. The concourse sidewalk got superheated, and after a while, I could feel the bottoms of my feet burning inside my sneakers.

By eleven o'clock, people were passing out. The soldiers still hadn't handed out any water or food, and every twenty minutes or so, Hancock picked up that bullhorn and hammered us with his voice.

Fess told Sergeant Scobie, "At least Moses was movin' when he faced his desert. You got us pinned down here bone-dry, and with all that water in the street, too."

"That water's got to be near poisoned from the sewers backing up and such," Scobie answered him. "Be patient. There are more supplies comin', and buses to take you outta here if they can get through the flooded streets."

"I don't care how nasty that water is," Pop told Uncle Roy on the side. "I'd make through it like a river rat to see what's left of our home."

"I'm with ya, Doc. But you heard what these soldiers said 'bout stopping anyone who wants to split," said Uncle Roy. "They might mean business."

"I'm not in any army—real or fake," Pop said. "I don't take soldiers' orders."

There were TV reporters on the concourse doing interviews and asking all kinds of questions. Two women standing right in front of them squared off and threw punches over who owned the last of some baby formula. The cameras were on them in a second, so the soldiers rushed in and broke it up quick.

"Maybe them soldiers wouldn't have disappeared last night if there were news cameras inside," mocked Fess.

And nobody argued.

The reporters found a man crying, holding a young boy in his arms. First they found out what his story was. Then they put him in front of the cameras to tell it on TV.

"The water came rising up so strong you couldn't stand," the man said, sobbing. "I got onto the porch roof with my son and was tryin' to pull my wife up, too. 'You can't hold me!' she was screaming. 'You can't hold me!' Then the current ripped her away. I don't know where she is. She's all I had in this world. Her and my boy."

Right away, I started thinking about Mom, and how it didn't take anything near that big to pull us apart. But at least I knew where she was—safe in Chicago.

That boy was staring straight down at the sidewalk the whole time, pretending not to hear. The reporter announced the woman's name and said if anyone had information about her to please call in. But when that TV crew walked away, I couldn't figure out if they'd done anybody any good, or just used that family's pain to keep people watching their channel.

Maybe fifty feet from us, a soldier tipped back his canteen and took a long drink in front of everybody. That's when a woman reached over the barrier and snatched the canteen right out of his hand.

"This isn't a prison camp!" the woman shouted at him, before she drank out of it.

People were laughing and hooting hard at him.

"Yes, ma'am!" hollered Fess. "I hear you!"

That soldier tried to suck it up, but he couldn't, and snapped all at once. He was about to jump the barrier to get his canteen back when a bunch of other soldiers, with their heads screwed on tighter, stopped him. Then Scobie got ahold of him and walked him off to a different section to stand guard.

When that woman was done drinking, she passed the canteen over to somebody else. Even after it was empty, people were holding it up high, waving that canteen like a trophy they'd won. Everybody was cheering for whoever held it. Then after the fuss died down and the canteen disappeared into the crowd, somebody chucked it overhand into a crowd of soldiers, crowning one in the head.

Fess pointed up to the sky and shouted, "*He* did it!"

Uncle Roy laughed like anything over it, but Pop wouldn't crack a smile.

"Command and control!" Captain Hancock screamed at his soldiers. "Command and control!"

I'd played football for coaches who yelled the same kind of shit. But once you were square in the middle of a real scrap, words like that didn't mean a thing. They were just more noise in the background.

• • • • • •

Pop opened his gig book and started calling off the names of clubs he'd played and people he'd jammed with. Uncle Roy and Fess had something to say about almost every one, like they were watching home movies.

"Here's a gig we did with Fess close to thirty years ago," said Pop, showing my uncle the page. "Look how he signed his name for me—*Mr. Lonnie Easterly.*"

"You stuck-up bastard." Uncle Roy grinned at Fess. "Is that what we had to call you by back then?"

"I probably said to myself, 'Look at these two genius boys. They can't remember who they're playing with 'less somebody writes it down for 'em,'" Fess crowed.

Pop pulled a pen from his shirt pocket. He turned the gig book to the first blank page, and at the top wrote, *August 29, 2005—Superdome—Funeral March for Cyrus Campbell.*

"I'll be a little less formal this time," said Fess, signing his nickname.

Uncle Roy signed it, too. Then I watched Pop write out his own name, and study all three signatures sitting together.

"That might be the last gig that gets into this book

for a long time," said Pop. "But it's the first with Miles on board."

So I grabbed for the book like it was a joke. Only Pop let it go, without fighting me. I couldn't believe how my hands were trembling once I had it. I held it steady and signed my name neat, so nobody would ever mistake it.

I signed—*Miles "Chic" Shaw—drum*.

"There, now I'm *official*—a musician bum like the rest of you," I jabbed at them.

But when I picked the pen up off the paper and gave the book back to Pop for him to see, something inside me started to breathe a little easier.

10

And when my hunger is all I have
When my hunger is all I have
Lord, how I want to be in that number
When the saints go marching in

Tuesday August 30, 2:30 P.M.

The hotter it got, the harder it was for people to hold on to their tempers. Everyone was angry at being stranded outside the Superdome, having to look up at that mother all day.

A white man got beat down by a crowd of people, and the soldiers had to step in and save his ass. They pulled him from the bottom of the pile all scraped up and bleeding, wearing nothing but a pair of blue denim shorts with the back pocket pulled inside out. Later, I heard it started because he asked to bum a cigarette off somebody. But everybody knew that him being white was a big part of it, too.

"I told you how it was gonna be," Pop said to me. "This is shelter life super-sized and pushed to the limit. Now they got us out here in the blazin' sun to boil up our blood. It's a wonder we don't all kill each other."

Helicopters buzzed over our heads like dragonflies, and their rotors sliced the hot air with a *thump-thump-thump-thump-thump-thump-thump*.

Lots of those copters landed on the other side of the Superdome. Some of them were bringing in people who'd been rescued from the flood, but others looked like they were hauling supplies. Everybody said it was food and water they were delivering, and people stood up on their tiptoes to see. But an hour later, we were still sucking our own spit, and our stomachs stayed empty.

A dude with a TV camera strapped to his shoulder was walking along the barrier, filming us. Some people stared straight into the camera and shouted things like "Save us, Jesus!" or "They sent us out here to die!" Others stuck up their middle finger or dropped their heads down in shame.

When that camera focused on me, I tensed up inside and felt like the whole world could see me stripped naked. I was about to turn around and look the other way when I figured Mom might see me and feel better to know for sure I was safe. So I looked into the cold black lens and saw the reflection of everybody around me—squeezed down small and stretched wide. I tried to keep my face blank and not show any expression at all. But I couldn't tell if I did.

After the camera passed, I turned to Pop. I could see the worry in his eyes that nobody watching TV would ever pick up on. I felt it, too. And right then, I would have traded a cheeseburger deluxe with fries and a two-liter Pepsi to see if our apartment and Pharaohs were still standing.

That's when a man jumped in front of the camera and shouted, "I don't treat my dog like this! Is this the Third World, or is this America? We need help!"

Then he turned to everybody behind him, and yelled, "Let 'em hear you everywhere—We need help! We need help!"

At first, just a handful of people screamed it with him. Then out of nowhere, something big kicked in. People started pounding their feet and clapping their hands to those words. All of a sudden, a good rhythm got going. More and more mouths opened. Pop, Uncle Roy, and Fess were chanting it, too. I went into our stuff and grabbed my drum. I pounded out that rhythm harder and harder, till it sounded like thunder in my ears. Then almost everybody stuck outside the Superdome started shouting those words.

"We need help! We need help! We need help!"

Hancock used his bullhorn, but nobody could hear a word of what he had to say. He was blocked out by our voices, and the captain's bars on his arm didn't count for crap.

Those voices wouldn't die down or quit, either. It didn't even matter about the TV camera anymore. I guess it was something that built up inside people so strong it needed to let loose. And for maybe ten minutes solid, the air was being rocked by that chant.

The stink from that sewer water in the streets got so bad it was like breathing into somebody's armpit. People all around us were pissing and shitting everywhere, and the concourse got turned into a giant toilet.

"The stench of death's mixed in there, too," said Uncle Roy, pointing to that old lady in the wheelchair I'd seen inside.

She was sitting on the other side of the barriers where the doctors were. Her face, and the rest of the top half of her, was covered up beneath a plaid blanket. I guess she never opened her eyes again, or maybe she did and couldn't stand what she saw. There wasn't going to be a march or music for her passing. Maybe no one here even knew her name. But I prayed her soul was sailing over that river in Africa with Cyrus's.

"Corpses are rottin' all over this city, I guarantee,"

Fess said. "There's probably even some in this jamboree here who look like they're sleepin'."

"So we shouldn't let you nap too long," cracked Pop.

"That's right. I want to wake up to your horn, Doc. Not the angel Gabriel's," said Fess, without a smile.

It was just past four o'clock when the first signs came that we were going to be fed. The soldiers set up stations, and people turned frantic, trying to get into line. Then Captain Hancock got back on his bullhorn, and for the first time people shushed each other down to hear him.

"We have secured water and emergency rations to sustain you," Hancock announced, stiff. "Remain orderly! I repeat, remain orderly!"

Even after standing in the hot sun all day and breathing in the same stink as we did, Hancock never dropped that army act for a second. I wondered if he was some kind of robot running on batteries, as I glared into the whites of his eyes. Then I thought about what his kids would be like after growing up in a house with him, and I quit right there.

Pop wasn't in the mood to fight for space on any line. So me and him got a spot more than halfway back from the middle, with Uncle Roy and Fess staying behind to guard our stuff.

Then Pop turned to me with a speech that had nothing to do with being hungry.

"Miles, I know I ain't been the best father there ever was. But I want you to know that I love you," he said. "Sometimes a man chooses a road and he can't turn back. He gets tied up to certain things and won't let go. So no matter what comes in the short term—if we get separated 'cause of anything that comes out of this storm—I want you to know I'm not cutting out on you."

"Why would we get separated, Pop?" I asked.

"I got to jump that barrier, Miles," he answered, serious as a heart attack. "I can't rest no other way—not till I see what's happened to my life. I spent it makin' music here. I can't get on no bus and just ride away for someplace else."

"That's nothing new, Pop," I said sharp. "You been ditching me for your music since before I could remember. So what's changed any? I got a drum I hit a few times now?"

"It's not like that, Miles," Pop said. "What I'm talking about's bigger than us."

"You go ahead. I won't hold it against you," I sparked, all fired up and sarcastic. "You *know* where it is you belong. I'm just finding out what that feels like. Only I ain't sure yet. Not like *you*, Pop."

He backed up a step and told me, "I can't fault you for what you said. But I can't fix it now neither."

Pop waved Uncle Roy over to take his place in line. Then he gave him his gig book to hold, and Pop pushed his jaw towards the barrier for my uncle to see.

But Roy didn't look too surprised or try to argue with him. Instead, he gave his lighter to Pop, who put it in his shirt pocket.

"I'll watch after Miles for ya, Doc," Roy said. "But don't do nothin' too foolish. It's bound to be brutal out there."

Pop walked over to where our stuff was. I watched him slap Fess's back and dig through the duffel bag for his horn. Then he stood by the barrier, eyeing the soldiers who were mostly getting people fed. Captain Hancock was busy barking out orders, but Sergeant Scobie was only twenty feet from Pop, looking over the whole scene. The three of them stayed that way for a few minutes, till I couldn't take it anymore. So I walked off the line and headed straight for Scobie, with my uncle calling after me low, "Miles, stay put."

"Sergeant Scobie," I said, like I had a question that couldn't wait.

He turned to fix his eyes on me, and when Scobie took the first step in my direction, Pop jumped the barrier and bolted.

Soldiers started blowing their whistles, and Hancock came charging over.

"Halt! Halt!" Hancock screamed after Pop at the top of his lungs.

Then Hancock grabbed for his gun, but Scobie bumped into him hard, probably on purpose. And Hancock lost his balance, falling down in a heap as his gun went flying.

That's when I jetted, too. I hopped the fence and flew past a soldier who only put a hand up to stop me. It took the first ten yards to shake the rubber from my legs, but after that I was really moving. I peeked back over my shoulder, but none of the soldiers wanted to chase us down in that melting heat, and they were just jogging after us.

I was closing in on Pop quick, but I couldn't catch my breath to call out his name, and he probably figured I was some soldier hot on his tail. He hit the end of the concourse ramp and was running toward the water in the street. Then I heard his feet start to splash through it. I geared down to look at it good and didn't know how deep that water was going to get. But when I reached the edge, I didn't hesitate and screamed, "Pop, it's me! Wait, Pop!"

11

Some say this world of trouble
Is the only one we need
But I'm waiting for that day
When the new world is revealed

Tuesday August 30, 4:36 P.M.

Pop didn't try to talk me into going back. He just looked at me like maybe I really did belong next to him. And the two of us pushed through that water together as Pop clutched the horn in its case against his chest.

"It can't be this deep all over," he said, with the water up to this waist. "That ain't possible."

"I don't know, Pop. I never been in a flood before," I answered, breathing hard.

Garbage, tree branches, roof shingles, and logs of what looked like human shit moved across the top of the water. It was cold as anything at the bottom, and my toes were turning numb. A photo album got caught up inside a little current, and was spinning in circles before I grabbed it to see. That water had slid a dozen pictures together, and stained some kid's first birthday party brown. I didn't want to see another page, so I chucked it behind me and kept on moving.

We hadn't gone far when we hit a dead body floating facedown.

"Don't get near it, Miles. He's probably got disease on him by now," Pop said, shoving water away with one arm.

The man had on a bright yellow shirt with a pattern of big red flowers, and shorts to match. He was dressed like he could have been walking on a beach in the Bahamas. But he wasn't. He was lying dead in a flood in New Orleans under a black rainbow of smoke.

After five or six blocks, the water level had dropped a few inches. The water was pitch black, and my body just disappeared into it. We were wading through it as fast as we could, and if the muscles in my thighs weren't burning from the strain, I would have believed the bottom half of me was gone.

Helicopters were buzzing everywhere. People were up on their roofs or hanging out of shattered windows. They were waving shirts and towels tied to broomsticks, trying to signal those copters to be rescued.

"I wanna get out of the line of sight from that damn

Superdome," Pop said, pointing to a side street with a red stop sign on the corner turned upside down. "The bigger streets are gonna get more attention. Nobody's draggin' me back."

There was a dog stuck up in a tree. He was balancing on a branch on all fours, barking wild like the end of the world was here.

Two grown men were pushing an air mattress towards us, with an older woman stretched out on top. She was tied to it across her waist by a bed sheet, and was almost unconscious. They said she was their mother—that she was a diabetic and they had to get her to the Superdome for insulin quick.

"They got doctors and nurses there," I said. "But it's crazy, too."

"We can't worry 'bout that," one of them said. "Police told us a three-foot shark got loose from the aquarium and is swimming somewhere in these streets. If that didn't stop us, nothing could."

Then Pop asked, "How is it behind you?"

"It ain't nothin' but hell back there," the other one answered, before they started moving again.

The water level was down to our waists, and the sun was so steaming hot, I thought maybe that flood was just evaporating.

A few blocks later, a boat showed up at an intersection. The man inside stood up to see us. He was wearing sunglasses and some kind of uniform, leaning on a long pole he used to steer. He waved us over, but we wouldn't go anywhere near him.

"Don't pay him any mind," Pop said. "Just keep on goin'."

I looked back one time and he was staring at us, shaking his head like he knew better than we did.

We climbed some concrete steps and walked out of that stinking shit-filled river onto solid ground. A family was camped out on a corner, cooking over a fire on the ground. I could smell the chicken frying, and my stomach started turning cartwheels. The father had a huge machete knife hanging from the front of his belt, and there were gunshots sounding from a few blocks over, by a row of stores.

He looked us up and down as we dripped a puddle on the sidewalk. Then he patted the handle on his knife and said, "You'd better be strapped with more than a horn if you're goin' into that mess up ahead."

Pop looked me square in the eye, like we were standing at those crossroads he told me about. I couldn't see any devil yet, promising me an easy ride. But I'd already heard Cain's empty screams. So I wasn't about to trade away my soul for anything.

"I've always made my own way, Miles," Pop said, like a warning. "I'm not used to worryin' over somebody else."

"Maybe I'm not used to being looked after by you," I answered him, pushing my feet into the ground till the water squeezed from my shoes. "But I guess you got a son to stress over now, and I got a Pop."

And we kept on going.

Plenty of buildings had been blown to bits—sometimes just one or two spread out on a block, like Katrina had took her pick. The ones made from brick were still mostly in one piece, and I pictured those three little pigs from the kid's story with their backs pressed up against the door to keep out the wind. Only this was no fairy tale you could close a book on and walk away from. And there wasn't any big bad wolf you could kill. It was something nobody could touch, not even an army of soldiers with machine guns.

"Look what that bitch did here," Pop said, pointing to a house that got picked up and shoved right through the one next door.

There was even an upside-down car, like a turtle stuck on its back, sticking out from under that whole mess. And both those houses were made out of wood, the same as Pharaohs.

We walked past that row of stores where the gunshots had come from. Only we were moving slow and cautious, like we were coming up on a hornets' nest. People were running in and out of the different stores with their arms full of stolen stuff. Katrina had cracked some of those stores wide open for them. But to get into the others, people had pulled down the sheets of plywood covering the windows and doors and smashed through the glass.

There were 'fros, fades, dreadlocks, cornrows, twists, and braids knocking each other senseless, trying to grab for all they could.

Lots of them were carrying out milk, bread, and other things to feed their family.

"Pop, if somebody drops a box of cookies on the floor, I might have to fight them for it," I said.

"I hear ya, Miles. My insides are starved for something, too," said Pop. "But I can't stomach what some of these bandits are making off with. Except for the food, it ain't nothin' but stealing."

Some people had their arms wrapped around TVs, or were rolling out shopping carts filled with radios, rugs, and cartons of car wax.

"It's everybody's store now!" crowed a guy, carrying away a whole metal shelf stacked with CDs and videos.

There was even a woman in the street trying on clothes she'd robbed, and tossing anything that didn't fit.

A bunch of cops were standing way off to the side, watching everything. There weren't enough handcuffs in a whole police station to arrest all those people, so they didn't make a move for anybody. But you could see how the cops were scared, too, and they never took their hands off the guns in their holsters.

Pop and me passed too close by an iron gate in front of somebody's house, and out of nowhere a man and his rottweiler charged the bars from the other side. The man swung a big claw hammer, and the dog was out of its mind barking.

We were so shook that we nearly jumped out of our skin.

"Nigger thieves—keep off my property!" the man seethed from behind the locked gate, with his black dog tearing his teeth through the air.

The man was white, and as old as Pop. But you could see by his twisted face that he'd snapped.

"Damn fool!" Pop exploded. "I'll shove that fuckin' hammer up your ass, you—"

That's when I grabbed Pop, pulling him away from the gate.

"Don't waste it on him, Pop. He's touched. Katrina musta pushed him over the edge," I said, with the most sickening tune I'd ever heard rattling through those iron bars as the man pounded them with the hammer—*piiing-piiing-piiing-piiing.*

After that, Pop needed to sit and settle himself, so he squatted on a steel rail outside a store. The sweat was pouring from his forehead, and I held his horn while he pulled his soaked shirt up over his face and then wrung it out.

The sun had already started sinking, but it was still blazing hot. I looked down for my watch and saw that it was gone. There was just the imprint of its face and the band left across my wrist. That's when a teenager broke out of the store, carrying away as much as he could. He was wearing a Saints football jersey and my eyes landed dead square on his.

"Yo, who you lookin' at?" he snarled, stopping in front of me. "Don't be eyeing my shit when all your sorry ass could snatch was some old trumpet."

I could hear Pop saying something to that kid, but I couldn't focus on what it was. There were a million thoughts streaking through my mind, and I wasn't sure which one would win out. Part of me wanted to lower my shoulder and knock that kid fucking flat. But another part wanted to break down and cry in front of him. Then one foot moved and the other followed, as I stepped to the side and out of his way.

"Yeah! Don't say shit to me," he howled, walking the path where I was just standing.

That's when we saw a crew of four Rasta-looking guys walking straight towards us, and Pop took the trumpet back from me. They were all wearing skullcaps with Jamaican colors—green, yellow, and black. And at first, I thought maybe they were with that loudmouth kid.

"There must be a reason you're out in these streets," one of them said. "'Cause I know you ain't here to play a concert."

Neither Pop nor me answered, and I fixed a hard look on my face to show we weren't going to roll over easy.

"Relax, young brother," he said. "This your father? You need food or somethin' to drink?"

They opened a bag full of bologna and bread they must have boosted from a store. Then they gave Pop and me each a sandwich and a bottle of beer.

"We're here to make sure nobody goes hungry and— if we can—nobody gets hurt," another one said. "Even if we gotta play like Robin Hood to make it happen."

People around us were calling them "Soul Patrol," and they even had formula and juice boxes to give mothers for their kids.

Pop sucked down that beer and told them how we were hell-bent for Pharaohs.

"You better make it before dark," said one of the Soul Patrol. "There might not be much love on the streets tonight."

A car came rolling by slow with its trunk popped open, and a man riding outside on the bumper. That guy jumped off before the car stopped, running up to some woman who was wheeling off a brand-new TV set in a shopping cart.

"You got to give that over, sister—law of the jungle," the guy snapped, shoving her down as she tried to fight him for it.

The Soul Patrol went running over to help her, and Pop and me followed behind out of shame. They didn't do a thing to stop that man from putting the TV in the trunk. But they made a human wall in front of that woman, so he couldn't touch her again. Only she didn't give a damn about being shoved to the ground, and just wanted that TV back.

"If I had a gun I'd fuckin' kill you!" she screamed, spitting at the car.

Then she cursed out the Soul Patrol for getting in her way and letting that guy make off with her stolen TV.

12

Oh, when the trumpet sounds its call
Yes, when the trumpet sounds its call
Lord, how I want to be in that number
When the trumpet sounds its call

Tuesday August 30, 6:18 P.M.

We kept moving, and on the next block there was a drugstore with a red spray-painted sign on its side that read, LOOTERS WILL BE SHOT ON SIGHT AND KILLED!!!

Two black dudes with shotguns stood watch on the roof. They had a homemade metal fort up there, too, in case somebody started shooting back. I guess they were the owners and didn't have a problem killing *any-body* who wanted to rip them off.

"Least they give fair warning 'fore they put a bullet in a brother," Pop said, sarcastic-like. "Most times you don't even get that."

People were emptying out other stores all around it, but nobody went anywhere close to that one.

We came up on a club where Pop had played plenty of times. It had big wooden shutters for doors, and the windows were boarded up with plywood. It didn't look like it was built any stronger than Pharaohs, and there wasn't a scratch on it. Other buildings on that same block had been smacked hard by the hurricane, but not that one. And I kept thinking how maybe somebody in heaven was watching down over it.

Pop walked up to it and stretched his fingers across the front door. Then he put his cheek to the outside wall, like it had a pulse he could feel.

"That's *one* still standing," he said. "But I know it can't all be good news."

Looters were everywhere, and any cops around just watched. Then a guy who was either drunk or insane went over to a group of cops by their car. He held his arms out to the side with his hands opened wide to show that he didn't have any weapon.

"You scared now 'cause these is the people's streets!" he hollered at them. "We the law now! Not you! Go hide! Hide from *your* crimes before the Mighty People judges you!"

The cops stayed cool for a while, letting him run his mouth. But then the guy put a big grin on his face and cursed their mothers for having them. That's when they pounced on him, pinning that guy to the ground.

Suddenly, shots started raining down from some-where—*Bam! Bam! Bam!*

Everybody ran for cover, including the cops, who left that guy sitting in the street with his hands cuffed behind him.

"Sniper! Sniper on a roof!" a cop screamed.

Pop and me hit the sidewalk, hiding behind the metal base of a streetlight that wasn't wide enough to shield either one of us.

I was scared shitless with those bullets buzzing around.

The cops were dug in behind their squad car, taking most of the fire. Maybe that sniper was only interested in picking off police. But those bullets bounced off the concrete, ricocheting in every direction.

The guy cuffed in the street stamped his feet and laughed out loud, like he was bulletproof and said, "Those is just mosquitoes to me!"

Then he looked over at Pop and yelled, "Stand up and play that horn, man, and I'll dance. You know these streets is made from music. Just close your eyes and play. You can find your way blind here if there's music in you."

Another round of shots rained down—*Bam! Bam! Bam! Bam!*

I could feel Pop's hand pushing on my back, and my

face going flat against the ground. I raised my eyes up to see, and the guy in the street was staring straight at me.

"Study your lessons, boy, before you get too grown to learn!" he cried.

Then the guy stood up tall and took off down the block. A minute later, the shooting finally stopped. But the cops never chased after him, not even to get their handcuffs back.

We got out of there quick, and Pop said, "That crackpot should play in a marching band. His brass balls are so damn big they probably clang together when he walks."

If my nerves weren't so numb from being shot at for the first time in my life, I probably would have laughed.

The shadows were starting to run deep through the streets, and we passed by a couple of clubs that took up pages in Pop's gig book. But this time the view wasn't so sweet.

Katrina had blown in the side of one place, and the roof had collapsed partway, too. We walked right up to where a wall once stood and looked inside. The wind had whipped around all the tables and chairs. Some of them got airlifted down the block, and others had smashed up against the stage and walls still standing, till they nearly turned to sawdust.

A clock in the back was frozen at a few minutes after seven—the time the current must have got cut off Monday morning. I was thinking how it must be about that time now on the flip-side, with the sun sinking down. Then I looked at my wrist, and the outline of the watch Mom gave me had already faded from my skin.

The second place was nothing but splinters. There was no clue left that a jazz club had stood there, and I wouldn't have known either till Pop sobbed over that spot.

"To see it now, you'd think somebody took up this space to sell firewood," moaned Pop.

"They'll build it back up again, even better," I said, as respectful as I could. "You'll see."

"There were spirits in buildings like these, Miles. They collected here over years and years," he explained. "I don't know if you can put *that* back together."

And I could feel something in my bones and blowing in the air all around me.

We were just a few blocks from Pharaohs when we hit a stretch of floodwater that rose ankle-high. There was a row of jazz joints coming up, and Pop held his breath to see them.

He stopped cold, staring down the length of that strip.

"Thank you, Lord," he whispered into the air.

Katrina had been almost kind to those clubs. Most of them were battered bad but still standing. I could see in Pop's face how tight he was over coming up on home. It weighed heavy on me, too, but deep down I was worried more about what it would do to Pop on the inside if Pharaohs was gone.

That's when two men looting the last club on that strip stepped outside. The first guy had a small piano hoisted up on his back, and had to be strong as a bull to do it. Then the second one followed, lugging a suit of armor with a silver sword wedged between its two hands in front of him.

I almost couldn't believe my own eyes to see them splashing down the street with those things. But when Pop saw them, he blew a fuse.

"That's the house piano from Santa's," Pop said. "It's been there close to seventy years. Some of the greatest cats ever laid their fingers 'cross those keys."

Pop went charging after that guy to stop him.

"Hey, you can't have that, man!" Pop yelled, jumping in front of him. "You put that piano back!"

"Get the fuck outta my way, old man, 'fore I drop-kick your ass!" the guy exploded.

But Pop wouldn't back off, moving sideways every time the guy with the piano tried to step around him.

"Yo, Clench, come slap this sucka for me!" the guy screamed furious to his friend.

The dude holding the suit of armor dropped it and took a step towards Pop. I knew there wasn't going to be anymore talking, so I hooked him hard under the neck, slamming him down—football style. Most bullies aren't looking for a real fight. They just want to be on the right end of a beating. But that wasn't going to happen. And I chased his ass halfway down the street, letting him disappear into the long shadows.

The other guy had put the piano down, and him and Pop were already wrestling. I steamed back there, pulling him off Pop. Then the guy wrapped both hands around my throat and tried to choke the life out of me. He was so strong I couldn't break his grip. He spun me down, pinning my shoulders to the street, and every time I wiggled free enough to catch a breath, I swallowed a mouthful of water.

Pop was on top of him, trying his best to get me loose. He was the only thing that saved me from getting suffocated and drowned at the same time. Then the guy pushed Pop off with one arm and tried to split my skull against the concrete.

I was desperate, fighting for my life and losing bad.

That's when I heard the first thud. Then the second.

The guy's grip loosened from my throat, and he slid off me into the floodwater. He was holding his head, screaming out in pain. He stood up slow and staggered away, with Pop waving his smashed-up horn at him, hollering, "Don't you ever put your filthy paws on my son again!"

I laid on my back, looking up at Pop.

"Miles! Miles! You okay?" he asked, frantic.

"Yeah—Pop," I answered, between gulps of air. "I'm still—in one—whole piece."

Pop had wrenched his knee, and lowered himself down onto the curb, looking at his bent trumpet.

"Is it all right?" I asked, concerned. "Can it get fixed?"

"There's still some good notes in her, no matter what shape she's in," said Pop, running his fingers over the valves. "I just couldn't lose you, Miles. Not for anything."

I saw the cardboard case with the red velvet lining floating in pieces in the street. Then I looked back at that horn in Pop's hands and knew for sure that he loved me more than his music.

I threw my arms around him, hugging him with all my might. There wasn't any space between us, and for once, every part of *me* felt close to *him*. Then I went over to that piano and knew I had to get it back where it belonged.

"I'm gonna get this done, Pop," I said, never more certain of anything.

I wasn't strong enough to hoist it on my back, so I had to pick it up and carry it a few feet at a time. I was straining like anything, but I wouldn't quit. It took me maybe twenty-five minutes to get it back inside that club, and I almost collapsed from exhaustion. But I felt a surge of energy rush through me near the end, and I finally did it, with Pop cheering me on.

"This city owes you somethin' for what you just done, Miles," he said, hobbling behind me. "It won't never forget, and I won't, either."

"That makes two of us, Pop," I said.

The sunlight was starting to really fade now, and I could see the outline of the shining silver moon. I had Pop grab on to my shoulders from behind. Then I lifted him off the ground and carried him the way a fireman takes somebody from a burning building.

We left that suit of armor lying facedown in the flood and started the last few blocks for home. I thought about that St. Christopher medal on the dashboard of my uncle's car. How he carried baby Jesus across that river and felt like he had the weight of the world on him. Pop had told me that he was the saint who looked after travelers. And right then, I prayed he was watching over us, too.

Neither one of us said a word as we turned the last corner.

Then we saw it.

Katrina had kicked the living hell out of Pharaohs, and our apartment had partly come crashing in on top.

Pop climbed down off me. He limped over to the cracked archway, pushing in what was left of the front door. He stared into the darkness, like he was searching for a ghost. Then he pulled out Uncle Roy's lighter to see by, and bent low enough to duck his head beneath a cracked beam.

I followed that light inside past our busted-up living-room furniture that had fallen through the ceiling, and the smashed bar from Pharaohs, till Pop found an open corner where the walls were still standing straight.

Then he got off his hurt leg and settled on the floor.

I watched his black face in the glow of the orange flame as he raised the trumpet to his lips with his free hand. He hit the first note and something inside me jumped. It didn't matter about the horn being bent or how it sounded. I felt the waves of music flowing through my veins.

Pop was playing that trumpet like he had nothing left in this world to lose.

I couldn't hold myself back, and didn't want to anymore. So I picked up a broken tabletop, pounding out a rhythm to match Pop's.

There was no stage left to play on, tables for me to bus, or kitchen where Cyrus washed dishes all those years. But none of that mattered, either.

Together, we raised the roof on that joint, and I didn't stop drumming till my hands turned raw.

I played my heart out for the spirits I sensed all around me—the ones that were tied to New Orleans, and could never leave or die.

Epilogue

We slept on the floor at Pharaohs that night. The next morning, soldiers on patrol brought us back to the concourse outside the Superdome. Before the day was up, Pop and me were put onto an evacuation bus for Houston, Texas. When we got there, the bus pulled up in front of the Astrodome, and Pop looked at me like it was happening all over again.

"I give it five minutes to be something different, Miles," Pop whispered. "If it's anything like the Superdome was, we're outta here today."

It wasn't.

There was plenty of food and water to drink. The bathrooms were clean. Families with babies and little kids had a special section. And everyone had their own cot to sleep on, too, with the space for it marked off on the floor. That all helped the soldiers and welfare workers in charge to run the show right, and there wasn't a single gang preying on people.

We found Uncle Roy and Fess inside of our first hour at the Astrodome. Pop and me just followed the sound of their jamming straight to them.

I finally got on the phone with Mom, and she wanted me in Chicago with her right away.

"As fast as I can get you here," she said, flat out. "If I need to wade through what's left of that damn flood myself, so be it. I saw that horror on TV. I can't sleep with you in another shelter. And where you gonna go to school? I've been worryin' myself sick since Sunday. I can't take no more, Miles. I want you with me."

"I love you," I told her. "And I miss you. But I can't walk out on Pop. Not now. We got somethin' goin' on together."

Pop wanted me in Chicago, too.

"It's probably best for you," he said, with his head hanging down.

But I wasn't going to leave him, no matter what.

A week later, we were still living in the Astrodome, and I was all set to start high school in Houston. Then Pop, Roy, and Fess got an offer to move to Seattle,

Washington, and play the jazz clubs up there while New Orleans got rebuilt. The Seattle Jazz Society sent somebody to the Astrodome to find musicians who were left homeless by Katrina.

The four of us moved into a house together there, and I started out in a new city and school without knowing anybody my own age. And it was hard.

Pop got himself a new horn and two trumpet cases.

Every time Pop played a gig, he'd have his bent horn sitting in an open case at his feet on the stage.

"Lots of folks find it hard to part with the past," Pop would tell the audience. "But this old horn reminds me that what you can't tear yourself from is *real* family."

I was too late for football tryouts at school in Seattle. But I got a spot as one of the team's equipment managers, and at least that kept me around the practice field with a football in my hands.

Everything wasn't perfect between Pop and me. We argued hard over my curfew on the weekends after I'd made a few friends, and about me getting a B-minus in music class. Pop still got caught up in his playing too much, especially living with Uncle Roy and Fess. But things were much better between us. And whenever I'd pull out the African drum Uncle Roy rescued for me, Pop would grin wide.

He told my uncle and Fess about me hauling the

piano back inside that club. That's when they stopped calling me "Chic" and my new tag became "River."

"You get called 'River' when you're part of the scene," Pop told me. "Lots of cats share that name, and what they got in common is they keep the flow going. They're part of the tradition that keeps the music rolling, and our heritage alive."

And I started to feel like part of that tradition every time I pounded the drum.

Then after we lived in Seattle for nearly seven months, the schools in New Orleans reopened, and Pop hustled us back home fast.

Uncle Roy had met a woman in Washington and wouldn't leave her behind.

"You won't be playin' at any wedding soon. I may be in chains, but I ain't a condemned man yet," Roy said, when he broke the news he wasn't going with us.

Pharaohs was in the middle of getting put back together. But there wasn't going to be an apartment on top of it anymore. That extra space was going to be part of the club now. So Pop and me moved into a government trailer, and Fess had himself one, too. There were rows of them all the same, put up for people who wanted to come back to work in New Orleans and didn't have any place to live.

Being there was extra tough, because everybody

around us was starting over from almost nothing. All they had was spirit and faith, and sometimes that didn't seem like enough.

In the first two weeks we were back, Fess got four offers from big investment companies to buy his property, even though Katrina had ripped the house on it to shreds.

"Of course, *they* want to buy," raged Fess the day we went over there to see what we could save from his place. "They wanna buy us all out. Pick up every plot of land they can from black folks while we're still tryin' to figure out which way's up. They'll try to get it for a song—whole blocks of blown-down houses. Then build it up for strip malls, luxury condos, or new hotels. Pretty soon there won't be any black faces livin' here. We won't be able to afford it. And that's what *they* want. Believe me."

"I take it you're *not* selling?" Pop asked him coy.

"*Not sellin'?*" Fess filled his lungs again. "Once I clear the front yard, I'm gonna pitch a tent there and live in it, just to make sure we don't disappear from these neighborhoods. And when I die, bury me with my clarinet right in the corner by the street, 'neath a big headstone for everybody to see. Then when those rich folks buy up the rest of them properties, they can walk with their noses up in the air, pretending not to smell my poor black ass."

I finished the last part of my sophomore year in New Orleans. Cain and Dunham were missing from school, and I never had to lay eyes on either one of them again. Football had been suspended the whole year because of Katrina. But that summer it started up again, and I made the varsity team as a tailback.

Then in late September, the Superdome reopened. The Saints took on the Atlanta Falcons in a Monday night football game, with practically the whole country watching. My coach had connections and got our team free tickets. Pop and Fess got a job playing in the stands that night for the crowd.

I didn't know how to feel as I passed through the turnstile. The newspapers said it took $185 million to piece the Superdome back together, like Humpty Dumpty. But no amount of gold paint could ever cover up what we went through in those seats.

"We probably played 'When the Saints Go Marchin' In' ten times durin' that game," Pop told me later. "And every time, I was thinking 'bout that march we had for Cyrus."

The Saints put a beating on the Falcons, winning 23–3.

I closed my eyes in the middle of that cheering crowd and could see Uncle Roy, Preacher Culver, and Cyrus and his family. I could still smell the stink and feel the heat rising, and the air getting heavy. I didn't want to ever forget what that felt like. What happened to us there was too important to let go of, or to give a free pass to anyone who helped cause it.

It was part of history now—part of *our* heritage.

I still don't know exactly where Pop and me will wind up, or if I'll ever be in that championship game. But I know we're part of something together—something that feels bigger than either one of us standing by ourselves.

And Pop and the rest of them can call me "River" all they want.